Anna Maria Ortese

The Iguana

Translated from the Italian

by Henry Martin

McPherson & Company

THE IGUANA

Published by McPherson & Company, P.O. Box 1126, Kingston, NY 12401.
Designed by Bruce R. McPherson. Typeset in Bodoni. Manufactured in U.S.A.
The paper is acid-free to ensure permanence. First paperback edition, issued
October 1988.
1 3 5 7 9 10 8 6 4 2

Library of Congress Cataloging-in-Publication Data

Ortese, Anna Maria.   The iguana.

Translation of: L'iguana.

I. Title
PQ4875.R8I313   1987   853'.914   87-20258
ISBN 0-914232-87-8
ISBN 0-914232-96-9 (pbk.)

This book has been published with assistance from the literature program of the
New York State Council on the Arts.

CONTENTS

The Man Who Buys Islands

I. A Stroll in via Manzoni   1
Daddo.

II. Ocaña   7
On the vast sea. An island in the shape of a horn.

III. The Meeting at the Well   13
The good Marquis. The Beast. Reactions to a scarf.

IV. The Miserable House   22
A discussion of the Universe. "Help me!"

V. The Involunatry Indiscretion   33
A madman. Hypotheses.

VI. The Stones   43
By candle-light. Nature in alarm.

VII. The Hat with Scarlet Feathers   60
A slow blush. To the hen house.

VIII. Daddo Disturbed   70
I saw you making piles of coins. The beast dreams.

IX. Ocaña's Two Moons   78
Another boat. Surprise!

X. A Family of the Universal Type   85
The archbishop.

XI. The Fear of the Devil   91
New hypotheses.

XII. Daddo Abandons the Closet   98
More coins. Daddo's dream.

The Storm

XIII. On the Beach   109
The voices behind the wall. Deceived! The good Cavalier.

XIV. Daddo Listens   117
A brief invitation to freedom. The definition of the diabolical

XV. The Little Star   126
Happiness. The fall. Abject dissimulations.

XVI. Daddo at the Cross-roads   134
"Even the sea has an ending." Salvato's high spirits.

XVII. Salvato Knows   142
Where the sky closes in. Packing up.

XVIII. A Strange Iguana   150
The colloquy. "The Virgin won't allow it!" In the hall.

XIX. The Terrible Mendes   157
A question for the unions. Absurd! Confusion.

XX. Daddo at the Well   165
The pretty little girl. Armed! On the trail of the culprits.

XXI. The Trial Begins   172
The hearing. At the well again. Almost November.

XXII. The Hearing Resumes   178
The high sky. Identified! Daddo content.

XXIII. The Voyage Resumes   183
Who the Iguana was. "Let's go ... the cosmos ... grace ... all of us...."

XXIV. The Chapel by the Sea   188
Letters from Ocaña. Winter. A crude invitation.

The Iguana

The Man Who Buys Islands

I

A Stroll in via Manzoni

Daddo.

Surely, Reader, you have heard already about the springtime travels of the Milanese, on the lookout all around the world for real estate, buying up tracts of land for the construction of villas and hotels, naturally enough, and maybe with working class dwellings to come a little later. But most of all, they hunt for still intact expressions of what they understand as "nature," believing it a mixture of freedom and passion, with not a little sensuality and a shade of folly, for which the rigors of modern life in Milan seem to make them thirst. Mixing with the natives or somber nobles of this or that island is one of the excitements most highly prized and eagerly sought, and if excitement strikes you as a target hardly congruent to the vast potentialities of money, then consider the strict correlation between financial abundance and the impoverishment of the senses. A strange obtuseness and general incapacity for discernment and gratification cloud the pinnacles of purchasing power, and many who come so far as to be able to sup on everything find relish in very little, if in anything at all. So they search out ever spicier flavors (which rather than spicy are really quite flat) and are ready to pay with their lives. All the Milanese may not fit this description, since most remain entrapped in business existences, still have not travelled or seen much of anything, and are equipped with only rudimentary curiosities; but it surely applies to a certain minority—the minority, finally, that gives the city luster. And imagination leads you astray if you think this minority not to include a few of those ingenuous, pure and rational spirits who show Lombard tradition at its best. Quite the contrary.

Don Carlo Ludovico Aleardo di Grees, of the Dukes of Estremadura-Aleardi and Count of Milan, though clearly of lineage two-thirds Swiss-Hiberic, was the finest and most debonair Lombard gentleman one could hope to find. Now in his thirties, the good Count Aleardi was an only son whose father's death had given him possession, while still quite young, of a sizable fortune sagaciously administered by his mother the Countess; and he combined an indistinct sense of ideals (likewise his father's legacy) with a passion for sailing and a less indistinct though reluctant attention to the intricate, ponderous dealings of his mother, who intended within the next few years to see an exponential multiplication of the young man's holdings, consisting primarily of buildings and property rights. He therefore set out every spring to look for sites where he would later build villas and yacht clubs for the summer amusement of the best of Milanese society. He was an architect. They had already purchased widely, and they intended (mother the Countess intended) to purchase still more. Daddo, however, as the Count was nicknamed, seemed really not to be interested. From somewhere or another, a Christian contentment had seeped into his blood and turned him basically indifferent to the very idea of possession, as though the true meaning of life had to lie in something else. In what, he couldn't have said, and his modest intelligence made it perhaps unlikely for him ever to be able to say, but he was already famous—Milan then had not yet grown so grey—for the calm, fresh laughter always ready to ring from his boyish mouth, no matter how slight the reason.

2

A party hidden to others, a music behind a wall, and some mysterious certainty of splendor and tranquillity seemed to be eternally within his reach and a constant reassurance, independently of youth, wealth, and name. He had not yet married, and had no marital intentions, even in spite of the pressures of his mother the Countess, who had already paid visits to several prominent Swiss families. He felt marriage would have limited him, yet one couldn't say how. He led the simplest life conceivable, the almost monotonous life of a monk. He spun out his days in his studio, drawing houses like a child, and his sole evening amusement was the company of Boro Adelchi, a young publisher of the *nouvelle vague*, extremely ambitious, but with still garbled finances. We'll add, parenthetically, that Daddo was careful to keep mother in the dark about constantly backing his friend with notable amounts of cash.

It was Adelchi, on one of those fine April evenings when Milan is all green and delicate and via Manzoni seems to stretch to no possible end, who cast the seed of our adventure.

In a somewhat pensive mood, Boro Adelchi remarked, "Well, no, things aren't going badly, but I'd like to get my hands on something really new, something extraordinary. We have a tremendous lot of competition. But you do a great deal of traveling, Daddo, so why don't you run me down something really first rate, something maybe even abnormal? Everything has already been discovered, but you never know. There are still a million possibilities. . . ."

"What you need are the confessions of some madman, how about the story of a madman in love with an iguana?" came Daddo's playful reply, and who knows how such a thing managed to enter his head? In fact he quickly turned silent and felt ashamed of himself for making fun of illness and the innocent lives of animals. Like so many Lombards, he felt enormous compassion for both, despite never having had anything to do with them.

"It's hard to say," replied Adelchi, missing that Daddo's quip had been intended as a joke. "What I have in mind would be more on the order of something poetic, say a series of cantos expressing the revolt of the oppressed. . . ." Then he too fell silent, but simply because he was reluctant to let Daddo realize he had no very clear ideas on the subject. That would have made him feel embarrassed, even though the Count was no better informed than he.

Here we have to offer a few words about a strange confusion that dominated Lombard culture at the time, thereby setting the tone of publishing—a confusion concerning the character of oppression and consequent revolt. Perhaps attempting to polemicize against the menaces of Marxist ideology, the Milanese saw oppression and revolt as no more than a question of feelings and the right to express them, forgetting that not even feelings survive—neither feelings nor any desire to express them—when people have no money (given the world's time-honored conventions), or where money can buy everything, or where penury cohabits with great ignorance. Briefly put, the Milanese were persuaded that some world of oppression had something to say, whereas the oppressed don't even exist, or can't, at least, have any awareness of being oppressed when their condition is authentic and a legacy from a distant past. The only thing left is the oppressor, who likewise has no knowledge of what he is, even while sometimes, out of habit, aping the stances and behavior that would legitimately befit his victim, if any such victim had escaped extinction. But these of course are sophistries that could never have assuaged the publishers' hunger for things with which to whet the public's languid appetite. Such arguments slow the rhythms of production. But to turn the issue upside down—an issue very fashionable at the time—and to

4

see oppression in frankly traditional and therefore reassuring terms, gave a fool-proof guarantee of approval, excitement, good will, and finally sales, coming again full circle to much-loved money.

Returning however to our two young men, serenely strolling down via Manzoni, and foremost to Daddo, since we're soon to see he wasn't seriously committed to his ignorance and possessed a generosity and purity of heart worthy of your full respect, here, Reader, is what he had to say:

"Well, we'll see . . . I'll give it a try. I imagine there's something illicit and full of suffering out beyond Gibraltar . . . I'll look around in people's libraries and bring back a manuscript . . . But I want you to make me a promise, Boro. You have to promise to print it without any splashiness; it has to be published for the moral improvement of the public, nothing else. Otherwise, there's no way I can help you." His smile was a little less playful than intended, and he slightly lowered his chin. His noble head was imprisoned by a veritable helmet of silver—the Aleardis always went prematurely, inexplicably grey—that sometimes gave his slender face an almost medieval gravity.

"Of course I'll promise. . . . You have nothing at all to worry about." Adelchi was excited and the lie came easily. His mind already rushed ahead, delightedly, to the next day's meeting in the conference room, even to how he'd announce the book in a few months' time from his penthouse offices. He'd give it a sensational title, like "The Nights of a Madman," or "The Witch," or better still, "Burn Them Alive!" Of course, he wouldn't actually read the book, being personally free of all morbid curiosity. He was really quite a simple man whose only burning passion was money.

By now they had reached the point in via Manzoni where someone proceeding from the Opera House has the Gardens on the left, the Gallery on the right, and the most beautiful

piazza Milan has to offer directly ahead against the background of a thinly-planted park that the fog, even in April,
wraps in a veil of tranquillity. The view affected Daddo as it
always did, and he felt a sense of loving sadness, as if the
scene were growing dark. He forgot his deranged discussion
of possible means for curtailing human boredom, and cast his
quiet gaze around him like someone in a dream which gives a
glimpse of counsels and prayers that the light of day wouldn't
allow to be taken as real. Behind so much peace was some
secret lament of the lost.

"Why should you imagine . . ." continued Adelchi.

But the Count was no longer listening.

II
Ocaña

On the vast sea. An island in the shape of a horn.

Two weeks later, having left his studio on via Bigli in the hands of two secretaries (one of whom, named Bisi, loved him to distraction no less for his being endowed with one of the most serene and lofty figures still to be seen on the Lombard plain), and after saying good-by to his mother the Countess who consigned him a good-sized emerald to be mounted in Seville by her most trusted jeweller, Daddo sailed from Genoa aboard the *Luisa*, a boat worth eighty million lire at the very least, setting his course towards the lower Mediterranean.

Unfortunately, like his mother the Countess on the values of life, and Adelchi where "oppression" was concerned, Daddo had few clear ideas when it came to real estate investment, maybe because he saw it as unimportant; and lacking clear ideas he could have no clear preferences. He knew the Mediterranean as he knew his own pockets, and almost all of it was for sale, yet he was plagued by continual hesitations. Sardinia, at times, would fill him with indefinable causes for perplexity, as though it still bore the weight of a yoke and needed protection rather than division into lots; or he would feel commiseration for the reefs and smaller islands off her coasts as though he thought them still too small to be separated from their mother (a ridiculous notion that might leave the Count accountable to charges of pietism if we weren't acquainted with his truly fraternal sensibilities). Or while admiring some of the most beautiful expanses of coastal Spain, he might seem to think that God Himself was watering the place with His tears and that nothing could be worse than opening it up to noisy tourists. It was a question of respect. Knights once undertook redoubtable adventures on behalf of women who inspired this subtle, slightly painful feeling of the dignity of others, and now this noble Lombard felt it, unknowingly, for the whole face of the earth. That very simple operation governed by the verb "to buy" never failed to present itself as a very complicated act for the Count to accomplish. But this time—who can tell why?—he found it even more thorny than usual. Only the gift of a light and well-balanced personality prevented him from beginning to fret. Trusting the able seamanship of Salvato, his sailor aboard the *Luisa,* he had already decided to sail through the Straits of Gibraltar, double the Cape of St. Vincent, and make his way slowly up the coast of Portugal, conceivably as far as the Bay of Biscay. He imagined he might sight some island belonging to no one, so buying it would cause no harm. In his simplicity he didn't stop to worry about the protests of his mother.

The weather was good, the sea calm, spring pressed warm breezes out beyond the coast to invade the open waters, and once, while the *Luisa* was moored at the delta of Rio Tinto as Daddo went ashore to find the Countess' jeweler in Seville, the blue of the sky was so blue it might have been cut into ribbons. Everything was calm and silent and being alive was a joy! In Seville, Senor Santos was away, having departed for a family gathering in Granada, and Daddo took advantage of his time by wandering among the city's narrow white streets, buying useless odds and ends. He knew they'd make a different impression on his mother and the secretaries, Bisi especially. One purchase was a white silk scarf with a fine gold filigree and very beautiful; another was a a necklace of blue-green stones for Salvato's wife so she too would have a happy gift when her husband came home. He also bought two cases of Malaga wine, which dear Adelchi would surely appreciate, and then a few postcards and pipe tobacco for himself. By sunset he was back in Palos, and the *Luisa* returned off-shore.

They sailed now for several days, if only because Salvato seemed to have made up his mind to furl the canvases whenever the breeze grew fresh. And the Count, always well-mannered and not much caring about schedules to maintain, let him do as he liked. All the days were much the same. Whenever he could Salvato would lie down and sleep, a forearm cast back across his eyes, and Daddo, whenever Salvato didn't need to be relieved, paced back and forth along the deck, filling his pipe, admiring the liquid-turquoise waves, smiling inwardly and thinking how the world, in spite of its never-ending question of Russians and Americans, is really such a beautiful place, and the Universe something gracious.

They reached Lisbon on May fifth, finding the city in the middle of some religious festival, bells ringing from cathedral towers and the people aswarm in the streets, gathering here and there at gaily-colored kiosks to buy peanuts, raisins, roast pig, plaster saints, toy trumpets and little wooden carts, yellow and green, harnessed to miniature white horses with red trappings, things that cost no more than a few *centavos*. The Portuguese were no exception to what people do everywhere at festivals. Daddo found them very fine people indeed, if just a shade touchy, and was sorry he wouldn't see more of them. Unless he sighted some new and unexpected anchorage, no other ports of call were planned before Coruña, where once again they would be in Spain.

The following morning, May sixth, as they continued to

sail in deep water off the western coast of the Iberian peninsula, in a sense the very edge of Europe, something changed. The weather was still good, but that startling blue had disappeared. The sun was different and its light seemed vaguely veiled, as though passing through scattered clouds. But the sky was clear. The sea too had lost its turquoise clarity and had taken on a hue of burnished silver, like the back of a fish: for scales a myriad of tiny waves moving in unison. There was a sense of great peace. No greater, perhaps, than in the Mediterranean (since the sea is everywhere the same), but that was how it seemed because of the pallid colors in which the sun had gone to sleep, leaving a sadness in the air, almost like Holy Week, even if this year's Easter had come very early and summer now was not far off. The horizon showed only a flush of amber light, yet there was still a leeward glimpse of the low, naked coast of Portugal until, shadow-like, it finally disappeared. From reddish the light then mixed with a livid green and the waves grew larger though still not rough. It was at one in the afternoon on May seventh, after another night of steady sailing in which still more miles had passed while leaving the scene unchanged, that Daddo, on the bridge with his mind full of hazy thoughts, turned his boyish gaze into the distance against the sharpness of the light and saw a spot of green and brown in the shape of a horn, or a broken ring. It was nowhere on the map, and he asked his sailor what it could be. At first it suggested a school of whales because its outline, small as it was, showed a series of humps. Salvato replied that while he might be wrong he thought it was the island of Ocaña. His answer, though—this is how he always was, out of laziness—lacked any air of coming from a person with a burning curiosity he might have the luck to satisfy. Quite the contrary!

"Ocaña! Such a lovely name," observed the Count, removing his pipe from his mouth. But he spoke these words because something about the name had struck him as unpleasant, even bitter, and made him feel compassionate. He added, faintly questioning, "I see it's not marked on the map."

"No, it's not on the map," replied Salvato, dryly and seemingly attempting to look in a direction where this miserable scrap of land would remain out of view. "It's not on the map because the people who make maps, thank God, are all Christians and don't much bother about things that belong to the devil."

"Don't you think those words a little harsh for people who have simply found an unfortunate place to be born?" remarked the Count with an open smile. "If the devil exists, you can be sure moreover that the good Lord loves him as much as you and me. And what makes you talk about the devil?"

It had also occurred to the Count that this island might go for a fairly low price if it proved to be surrounded by some evil legend; and that, after all, would be nothing to be unhappy about. The Lombard mind always rests on a bedrock of practicality, and this too, in some way or another, is one of its virtues.

Faced with a question so squarely put, the sailor replied with little more than a grunt and a few half-formed phrases, inadvertently making it clear that the legend owed more to his laziness than to any foundation of historical fact. Salvato's shiftiness nonetheless nourished an impression which the Count was beginning to perceive as not too far from the likely truth. Rather than any normal island, which would have appeared on the maps, devil or not, this was probably no more than a desolate outcrop of reef, semi-arid and barely above sea level. Nothing would be alive there except roots and snakes.

"We'll see," he concluded.

This was not a good idea, but sometimes Daddo was like

11

that. Something in his character would stick and force him to look for trouble. Or, to put it more clearly, desolation and terror sometimes attracted him precisely because of his love for their opposites, as if he heard voices crying out sadly in the distance for help. It would take them out of their way, but Daddo instructed the sailor to steer a course towards the island, and the young man obeyed, though unwillingly.

They sailed for another half hour. Then they could see a few oak trees, a small field, and a house swimming dimly into view as through a pane of yellow or smokey glass. They continued to advance; a small group of people was sitting in the shade of one of those trees: a few men, and an old woman busy with her knitting. They had noticed the Count's luxurious yacht, but no one turned a head. One of the men, the youngest, with a head of hair like whitish gold, was reading something aloud, seated closest to the tree. The others listened silently.

Daddo waved, but his gestures went unanswered. The water now was shallow, and he told Salvato to drop anchor. He lowered the life-boat, the *Luisina,* and rowed across the remaining hundred yards separating him from the beach.

He would have said, who knows why, that the people beneath the tree were petrified.

III
The Meeting at the Well

The good Marquis. The Beast. Reactions to a scarf.

"Hello," he cried, "Can I be of any help?" and then felt immediate embarrassment at his clumsiness. Silence was the only answer Daddo had received, and he had no one to blame but himself. He had silenced these people by speaking in his native Lombard dialect, a language they could hardly be expected to understand. So, even fleetingly to have seen them as hostile or wary was completely unjust. All the same, Daddo felt vaguely apprehensive for a moment, sensing their silence, accidental as it was, to be a curious rhyme to their sad and bizarre appearance—bizarre at the very least—and to the strangeness of their occupation. The ocean, weighty and aglitter with light, lay spread out all around them while they turned their attention to some poem or novel, one of them reading aloud to the others. Daddo also felt, due perhaps to having been so long at sea, that the island itself, though almost imperceptibly, was moving. Rowing ashore, moreover, he had landed at a spot from which the *Luisa* could no longer be seen; the sea had closed in behind him like a great everlasting wall.

Meanwhile, however, as if to show how certain sensations are spun of nothing and how suspicions and perplexities can finally prove unfounded, the youngest of the men (at the center of the circle) had understood the visitor's predicament.

He stepped slightly aside from his natural podium—by now the old woman was on her way back to the house—and he quickly moved forward with a welcoming smile.

He was surely no more than eighteen years old, yet everything about him spoke of authentic but already ruined beauty. Tall and thin as a marsh crane, he had a long, narrow, Hyberean face, but the clear eyes and straight, fair hair of the English. He was dressed, like the others, in poor, colorful clothes of a cut that had long since ceased to be fashionable, but the colors themselves were strikingly different. The others' clothes were dark green or blue and gave a general impression of violet, whereas his own were light: a vest of yellow velvet, pale blue trousers again in velvet, red socks, and a shirt of green cotton, very worn and elaborately embroidered. On his feet a pair of the vilest slippers. The face and hands that issued from these sumptuous fabrics— sumptuous though tattered by moth holes and creased by years of constant use—were just as delicate and consumed. They also bore a touch of something ingenuous, timid, and volatile, something even joyous despite their pallor. As he approached, he grew constantly brighter, like the bank of a stream as the sun evaporates a mist, and the Count could see that the transparent skin of his face was laced with a network of fine, short wrinkles like the nervatures covering the petals of certain flowers. For so young a man, he gave a strange impression of decrepitude and resignation. He came to a halt only a few steps in front of Daddo, inclined his head just barely, and introduced himself in an antiquated Portuguese so genteel as to seem almost womanly: don Ilario Jimenes of the Marquis of Segovia, Count of Guzman, and, aside from his brothers, the island's sole inhabitant.

Aleardo was frankly moved by the way this rush of boyish simplicity had relieved him of the traveller's customary duty to present himself first, and he quickly recovered from his initial surprise to bow in turn, give his name, and thank his host for so much affability. Daddo spoke Portuguese quite well, having often spent time in Brazil. He continued to relate that he had been sailing for several days with the idea of reaching some place entirely new, but had almost given up hope, considering the amplitude of current navigational knowledge. Fortune had come to his aid.

Don Ilario's smile was calm and pure as he listened to Aleardo, and then he replied, "That's a very kind thing to say of us, *o senhor*." His voice had a tinge of melancholy as he added, "This land is very dear to us, but it's not on the map because of its size. It is just that small. And it has no right to fly any nation's flag. Nonetheless we think of ourselves as Portuguese. That's what our family was when we came here from Lisbon in the 1600's. Now, however, I'll show the way if you'll be kind enough to follow me."

At that, don Ilario led Aleardo towards the house: a one-storey construction, ugly and grey, with a small tower against one side. Partly from how within the last few minutes the sunlight appeared further to have failed, much as in springtime when rain is due, the building struck the Count less as a house than as a stage prop. It left him feeling bemused. And when the brothers stood up to greet him, Daddo was impressed by how long and thick they were, how completely different from the younger don Ilario; they might have been born of a different mother. Their faces, moreover, were fixed and dispirited, and Daddo thought to have grasped why life might not be overly rosy for the good Marquis.

These two men seemed more like servants or field hands than gentlemen, and after introducing themselves as Hipolito and Felipe Avaredo-Guzman, the sons of an Asturian first wife of the late Marquis, they lapsed back into speechlessness: the very same apathy with which they had listened to their brother as he read to them, and Daddo was quick to

15

recognize its source. They were coarse and taciturn by nature, and what little imagination they possessed was slow and leaden; but that wasn't all. Their apathy was equally the fruit of the economic desperation in which they all too obviously lived. Poverty was more forgiving to the candid don Ilario, who could discover some solace in a love of literature.

The lives of Hipolito and Felipe Avaredo-Guzman were a desert, and they knew it. They were consigned to decrepitude and aware of having no issue. The attention given to their brother's reading could hardly be called attention at all. It was the behavior of men on their death-beds, incapable of swatting a fly. Daddo saw it all quite clearly and was already turning matters over in his mind, already trying to imagine how this island might benefit from his wealth. These men could revive and flourish like plants, and he could offer the sensitive don Ilario a far more appreciative audience, even fame and recogition if he deserved it. Daddo thanked heaven for having made him Count of Milan, and his mother for having pushed him, with her endless ambitions, towards this unfortunate patch of earth.

Of all three brothers, only don Ilario gave sign of deriving any pleasure from this visit from abroad. Like Daddo he was young, and they were further bonded by the courtesy, nobility, and sensitivity they shared. He continually brightened and appeared almost to wonder how to prolong this visit; in fact, such an opportunity presented itself while walking Daddo around to see the rest of the island.

Just behind the house rose a low hill, surrounded by the oaks that had looked like whales when sighted from the sea, oaks that protected the island's solitary inhabitants from the assaults of the ocean winds. The hill itself was a pasture, unplanted and left simply as the open expanse willed by nature. There were a few sheep, some lying in the grass, some grazing, heads low, and, like all sheep, thinking perhaps of nothing. Farther to the right, in a hollow where wind and sun excited the silver tints and musical instincts of a grove of olive trees that shivered against the dazzling horizon of the sea, stood a well. Busily at work next to the well was the "little old woman" who had returned to the house shortly before, seeing that visitors had arrived. She must have gone out again through some back door.

Daddo's surprise was tremendous. He had taken her for a shrunken old woman, but he was looking at an animal! In front of him was a bright green beast, about the height of a child—an enormous lizard from the look of her, but dressed in woman's clothes with a dark skirt, a white corset, old and shabby, and a multicolored apron clearly patchworked from the family's stock of rags. To hide her ingenuous little snout, which was a sort of whitish green, she wore yet another dark cloth on her head. She was barefoot. These clothes reflected her masters' puritanical spirit and were considerably in her way, yet she seemed quite capable of everything a house-keeper has to do and of doing it with a certain speed.

Now however she was having trouble. One of her small green claws was bandaged, and she breathed laboriously while attempting with the other, in vain, to draw a large bucket up from the well.

Chivalry was one of the qualities that made Daddo so likable, and he didn't even stop to ask himself, as his religion would have told him to do, if this creature were Christian or pagan (the latter more likely). He went over to the beast and took hold of the bucket as she looked up into his face with two tiny eyes full of dreams and supplications. She murmured:

"Thank you, *o senhor*, thank you!"

"You're more than welcome, little grandmother; there's no reason to thank me at all."

"Yes," remarked don Ilario, "the rope is broken," betraying not the slightest concern over the impression such a servant might make upon his visitor. His tone was calm and relaxed, entirely free of embarrassment, and Daddo felt instantly reassured that there was nothing to marvel about in this "little old woman." Or, if there were, it was simply a part of the world's normality. The world itself, after all, is fairly enigmatic: at the beginning it wasn't there, and then it was, and no one has any idea where it came from. Daddo achieved such feelings easily, aided not a little by an instinctive leaning towards the ecstatic. Whenever he considered the workings of nature, he saw a soul no different from his own and heard it appeal for brotherly solidarity. For a fact, moreover, the creature appeared somehow downcast and perplexed.

Daddo quickly went about pulling up the other bucket too, careful not to look at the beast with any special curiosity since he wanted her to feel no embarrassment. Then, as the Marquis expressed his gratitude, he remarked that the broken rope could easily be repaired. He'd be happy to take care of it and had only to return to his yacht to fetch everything required.

A short time later he was back aboard the *Luisa*. He said nothing about what he had seen to the superstitious Salvato, and loaded the *Luisina* with rope and tools and as much as possible of everything else: a case of Malaga, Italian novels as a present for don Ilario, and the silk scarf filigreed with gold, which was truly folly as a gift for the poor old servant. The creature after all was female and Daddo was sufficiently unspoiled to imagine that some trace of vanity still had to be alive in her, despite the wretchedness in which she lived. He was far from wrong.

When the iguana—she was in fact an iguana—saw this pure and candid symbol of European culture spread out upon the blackness of the huge kitchen stove, she clasped her little fore-claws together (you remember that one of them was bandaged) in a gesture of mute and anguished admiration, and uttered a high sharp squeal that trailed out into a wail. A tear descended from her mild, imperceptible eyes, hidden eternally behind wrinkled lids. Actually the tear had to rise, since her eyelids, like those of all iguanas, opened exclusively from the top. The only comprehensible words among the confusion of her mutterings were:

"*Nâo para mim . . . Nâo para mim . . .*"

"But that's where you're wrong, little grandmother; it's for you and no one else," replied the Count as don Ilario smiled enchanted admiration at his new friend. "You see," Daddo continued, "it makes you look like a girl again! It suits you perfectly."

Unstudied words can spring up from the unconscious laden with some truth the rigid mind hasn't been able to grasp, and Daddo's remark brought him to a sudden, astonished realization. The creature he had addressed as "little grandmother" was not even a full-grown girl! She was still a child iguana no more than seven or eight years old who looked aged and dry only because of the typically wrinkled features of her species and a general decline, caused no doubt by carrying weights, constant serving, and who knows what state of savage loneliness too much for any youthful creature, even a beast. Now she was animated by a joy that showed her for what she was.

In a sequence of small, jerky movements that any observer other than the benevolent Count would have found grotesque if now disgusting, the creature arranged the scarf on her head, bending forwards and sideways to knot the two ends, just as a woman might do before a mirror. To look at herself, she had run up to a great copper pot her own green hands had polished to a shine. She leaned to one side and bent back her wrist as she raised a paw to the side of her snout, making much the same gestures the Count had seen performed by young ladies of high society on receiving the present of some costly rag. She turned to look at the Count with a face so radiant and yet so humble as almost to bring him to tears. He himself then looked towards the Marquis, hoping to see that handsome, finely-graven face come alive with feelings similar to his own, but that hope went disappointed. Rather than affection, the Marquis' face revealed a forced and distant benevolence as though the creature had caused him some grievance and deserved to be acquitted with rebuke as soon as they should find themselves alone.

"That's enough now, Estrellita; I want you to go to your room; the Count and I have things to talk about." Don Ilario's words were gentle but firm.

"*Nâo... nâo... nâo...*" and a confusion of other phrases in the language of Camões became a babble in the mouth of the creature, something whining and afraid. The sounds seemed trapped and bundled up within the whiteness of the scarf, but accompanied by a ringing of desperate little bells so silvery that the Count looked about to see where they were.... Then the Iguana was gone. She had disappeared rapidly through a trap door at the side of the stove and down into her "room," which must have been a cellar or a woodshed just beneath the kitchen. The door slammed shut, but a crack along its fitting with the floor tiles revealed the hole to be so completely dark as hardly to be a room at all and more like a dark and secret dungeon. Her muted "*nâo... nâo... nâo...*" rose up through the floor, sounding almost tearful. It was the voice of a disobedience even possibly chronic, which was something, in so young a creature, that might have been handled with greater patience. But the Marquis' face showed neither patience nor pity. His benevolence seemed to collapse into tacit, cruel impassiveness, then again to dissipate into a parody of a smile as his sweet voice returned:

20

"Yes, I have to admit that our Iguana is a little nervous. . . . Later, Count, I'll tell you where we bought her. You know, she is really very good, aside from being highly strung, and I have no idea what would become of us and this house if it weren't for the help of her aged hands. . . ."

"You bought her? . . ." asked the Count, and then stopped short since the emphasis in his voice and limpid eyes was so sharp that anyone at all, let alone a sensibility so exquisite as don Ilario, could intuit what was surfacing into his feelings, if not yet into his mind. If the Iguana had been bought, she could be bought again and he could restore her not only to her freedom, but as well to all the dreams of her little bestial soul. The Marquis, however, reacted to the question as though he had only heard a gust of wind or the murmur sometimes made by the sea. Daddo's query went unanswered.

IV
The Miserable House

A discussion of the Universe. "Help me!"

On leaving the kitchen, don Ilario led Daddo on a tour
through the rest of the house, which proved much larger and
more beautiful on the inside, even in spite of its shabbiness
and sadness, than might have been guessed from out of doors.
Any number of rooms, including the entrance hall, splayed
off from a long central corridor and the Marquis meticulously
showed them to his visitor, one after the other, though never
offering more that a glimpse through doors pushed open just
a crack. All of them were awash in dark, indescribable abandon, and their high white walls shimmered with reflections,
filtering up from tiny grainy-glassed windows, of the myriad
movements of the foliage of one or two trees outside, shaken
in the silence by the sun and wind. Dusty books, run-down
clocks, bunches of tomatoes hung up to dry, a few family
portraits, green cupboards with unhinged doors ... everything usual in old neglected houses, but here in great abundance and contrasting unaccountably with the Marquis'
claim that the Iguana busily attended to chores and kept the
house well-ordered. No, there was no such thing as order
here, something even that made order impossible, and the
Iguana's employment as housekeeper was simple appearance. Faced with such inconsistencies, which began to con-
strue a fairly sinister outline, the Count ever more frequently

22

wondered what mystery the house concealed, and whether poverty was its sole or worst affliction.

At the end of the corridor, where one of the typically narrow and curtainless windows flashed momentarily in the sunlight just breaking out from behind a bank of clouds, one could see how the hallway elbowed and then continued along the entire right side of the house before finally halting in front of a narrow stone staircase which rose into the tower that adorned the dwelling, seen from outside, like some great decay-riddled tooth. Dust and broken steps here again, but with an added acrid odor of years of accumulated paper, and a musk of rotted ink, smells in some way familiar to the Count. Linked with the scene he had found upon landing, they revealed the young Segovia's true occupation. He was a poet, perhaps a bibliophile, at any rate a spirit immersed in eternal fantasy. Remembering Adelchi's request in Milan, the Count resolved to seize the earliest opportunity to inquire if he might not have some interesting manuscript.

"Here," don Ilario was meanwhile announcing, "is my library," pointing out the direction with his transparently ivory hand. "I'll show it to you later . . . right now it needs a little tidying. I do hope you'll spend the night here, and maybe pass the day with us tomorrow. That would make me very happy! You can't begin to imagine my gratitude, Daddo! Now, however, you must be tired, and I should show you to your room."

Every one of these phrases seemed to open onto the vista of a weakness; they revealed a flaw, vulnerable and unprotected, and a trace of something ecstatic as well, as though the salutary presence of the Count had suddenly led the young Marquis to a nascent forgetfulness of all the evils that afflicted him, everything that troubled or annoyed him. His heart might have been disclosing itself to some much-loved, undying hope, long submerged but ready now to resurface.

After resting in his room for perhaps half an hour, if rest is any way possible within already perfect repose—for the Count had never before felt more relaxed, almost as though enveloped within the delicious half-sleep of an early April afternoon, and his entire surroundings lulled and cradled him at much the same time that he found them disquieting— Daddo was quite happy, at the sound of a light knock on his door, to get up and go to join his hosts, already seated for lunch. They ate in the big dining room and were served by an Iguana quite different from before. Not that she wasn't the same Estrellita who had reacted to the scarf with such large and incomparable felicity and almost with a flowering of sud- denly resurgent youth, but it was now as if some ancient humiliation—the secret of which may have lain in that re- proof from don Ilario—had once again clouded her pain- filled mind, and she seemed to have decided, even in spite of her love for the Count, not to rise from the abyss of the most apathetic submission, the most dejected somnolence of the heart. She placed the dishes on the table indifferently, al- most impolitely, much as the Count had sometimes observed in the behavior of unhappy children; and afterwards, appar- ently bored, she went to lie down on her mat beneath the table, where don Ilario occasionally threw her a bone or a piece of skin from the chicken Felipe had prepared for the guest. There was also potato soup, flavorless and with the potatoes unpeeled, but the Count understood that Felipe had done his coarse best; so he repeatedly tendered his compli- ments, saying he had never tasted such a soup before (a truthful remark) and intended to instruct his cook to add it to the menus of his meals in Milan. Excepting the lack of a single thing, nothing would have kept the Count from feeling perfectly serene and at ease, perhaps even truly happy. If only these provincial nobles had permitted their bestial ser- vant to take a seat at the table and made some attempt to assuage the hurt he could read behind the carapace of her pitiful forehead! But no possibility could have been more remote; and Daddo knew it, which did nothing however to diminish his own pain, especially since she crouched on the floor right next to his chair, and from time to time he spied her little green paw outstretched from beneath the table to beg a few crumbs or a crust of bread. Her tiny eyes were red and bloodshot, and her clothes and appearance all untidy and awry. A foglike obscurity had settled about her long slender snout, resolutely trapping her suffering or resignation—one couldn't tell which— within a total incapacity for expression. Entirely abandoned to herself, she seemed at times to have fallen asleep.

Marshalling all of his strength and good breeding to ignore the Guzmans' cruelty and the gravity of its offense to his sensibility, the Count turned the conversation to the second of the purposes of his voyage and said nothing of the first; the notion of purchasing islands for his mother might easily have abraded the feelings of these unfortunates. His subject was the florid development of Milanese publishing and how the lack of new works might at some point threaten the whole industry with collapse and bring the wheels of its machinery to a stand-still. He spoke quite highly of the young Adelchi, after duly praising the efforts of the other publishers too, and remarked that a radiant future could easily be predicted for his friend, if only because of his brilliant and inexhaustible gifts in scouting out and buying up new talents. To round the discussion to a finish, he then disclosed the request Adelchi had made of him during that evening in via Manzoni, shortly before his departure. Here again he was careful. While revealing his ambition to take back some unpublished manuscript of stories or cantos concerning Portugal, he omitted any mention of the subjects current fashion suggested as most suitable. To say his market was interested in poverty, oppression, and if possible in treatments of the spicier modulations of love, wouldn't have shown much tact in a house where the first and second overflowed, and where the third, even in its most bland and normal forms, seemed entirely unknown. He limited himself to suggesting that a work by the master of the household might just fit the bill.

As don Ilario listened to the Count's proposals, his sad blue eyes once again filled with those lights of joy and hope that Daddo had noticed when they had talked in the corridor, but he offered no signs of response to so bold a suggestion, almost as though his much troubled mind (which is to what prolonged and unpunctuated solitude will lead, when not, as we shall see, to true and proper deliriums within parentheses of sudden, shattering calm) didn't dare to linger on such possibility. Perhaps, argued the Count, he preferred to postpone discussion until some moment when his interest might assert itself more casually. He would steer such a course not from any self-serving calculation, but rather because of the intensely-experienced modesty by which elevated spirits are always plagued when faced with any hint of an opportunity for material gain. When don Ilario told Estrellita to bring in coffee, but first to go to his room to fetch the novels the Count had given him, he seemed almost to be laying the foundations for a curiosity that might later, in respect of all decency, connect the query to a reply. The little servant, sad and mesmerized, crawled out from beneath the table and obeyed, going off to do her errand, but not returning so quickly as to prevent the Count from making a discovery. He picked up the interrupted conversation, cautiously interrogating don Ilario on the conditions of Portuguese culture, and soon found that the boy, when faced with the word "culture," held an attitude that struck him not a little, and unfavorably.

The Marquis observed that he surely had no right to

overlook the contrasting economic conditions that differentiated the two countries, Italy and Portugal—bringing the one to the fore, as it were, and leaving the other considerably behind—but that this, for as much as he could see (and here, he added, he might be wrong but felt better off if not) was fairly irrelevant to any real explanation of the delay, in Portugal, of an artistic and literary renascence, and thus of the enterprise of publishing. It was rather that the Portuguese spirit, though somnolent, harboured a deep and painful awareness of the dualism at the base of Creation and was firmly established in the conviction that as good increases, so too does evil; this latter, however, being stronger than the first and capable of pressing every work, action, and progress of good into brightening its own contrary fire—as might easily be confirmed, he insisted, by surveying the current conditions of life among the various peoples of the world. In other words, since all good served as incentive for evil, as further encouragement that it raise its gnarled and frightful head, the very greatest act of piety had to lie in abstention from all good—so that life itself, a compound of good and evil, might slowly and finally perish, dissolving at last the lymph of this entanglement and allowing whatever force or forces responsible for the original error to correct themselves, change their systems, and then reconstruct a world from which evil would be totally excluded. This, demonstrably, being the true goal of culture—the deliquescence of life and the affirmation of its resurrection by returning through the primal void—it was clear, he said, that the truest road and proper task of every man of feeling or poetic genius was to damp down his breathing to a minimum, or at least to conceal it, so as not to blow upon the flames of a maleficent creation, full as an egg with crime and unspeakable deceit.

Though the Marquis spoke these words with the air of establishing some initial mystic paradox or a premise some-

where between the playful and the deranged—from which
the discourse might then be thrown quite frankly onto more
concrete terrain—something in his eyes made it plain that
this concept of the world and this overweening fear of evil
were far more serious presences than polite conversation
would allow him to express. At this very moment—and perhaps it had been like this for years—simply for him to mention them was enough to drag up a spectre to the back of his
chair; and they terrified him, just as prankish poltergeists
make game of defenseless children. For an instant he flushed
deep red, and when the color had fled again from his face, his
eyes remained weighted with some stony, atrocious fixity. It
was painful, too, to see how alone he was beneath the crush
of his depression. The Avaredos, at either end of the table,
continued their meal as though nothing had happened, even
exchanging glances of satisfaction over their tasteless gruel
as they stirred it around in their plates with broken forks and
slopped it over crumbled hunks of bread; bending their wooly
heads low over the table, they shoveled these morsels into
their mouths, and the silence resounded with noises of their
enjoyment.

"Forgive me, Ilario," the Count now remarked, seeming
to return to himself after a deep, brief voyage, "but at this
point, if I've understood, you'd deny that the course of the
created Universe, and even the very act of creation, is in any
way a fulfillment of a mission of love."

"Not exactly," responded the Marquis, "but I'd say that
God, or what we refer to as God, isn't the only origin of things.
Look at nature itself, and it seems the unhappy outcome of
two different elements as they mix and interplay with one
another, the one active, the other passive, or, if you prefer,
the one positive and the other negative."

"But I see no evil in that."

"You see no evil in everything that throttles life, life

and every sublime aspiration to identify with the Supreme? You see no evil in what reduces our existence to a rat trap?"

"Not as I see it," replied the Count, "if precisely this evil allows the gift of life to reveal itself. Surely," he calmly admitted, "there's something strange in this architecture that surrounds us and never ceases to expand, if only, among other things, because we can't discern its foundations; but we have to leave it at that. This construction, my friend, is a very great good, and I hope you can find the strength to believe me. You see it shot through with pain, but this pain is a part of the process that constructs it."

"In that case, I am the dreamer!" responded don Ilario, with bitter sarcasm. "It's only my personal fantasy that evil exists and oppresses us." Then, in a murmur, "You'll have to excuse me. I have the feeling it's terribly hot in here... but cold at the same time." His face wore a bizarre expression, anger mixing with fear, and his hands visibly trembled as he opened the collar of his shirt.

"Porqué o tempo esta mutandó," commented Hipolito, with the attitude of having come up with a witticism.

Moved by the younger man's suffering, but more so by this whole discussion of good and evil and the meaning of the Universe (such topics of conversation had always attracted the Count and were no longer really permissible in Milan), Daddo reached out to grasp the Marquis' cold hand and pressed it into his own.

"You know, my friend, there's surely nothing futile in anything you've said, and I'm grateful for your thinking me worthy to listen to you. But some day, as you'll see for yourself, you'll think of certain fears as laughable. Once you free yourself of this tremendous sense of solitude, you'll discover that the world, when it isn't ill, is good; and what's needed to heal it when it's ill is our capacity for intelligent love."

As soon as these words had been spoken, the hand

Daddo held in his own momentarily relaxed and responded, almost overwhelming him at having gained so much trust, and the eyes looking up to his might have belonged to a newborn child, trembling between tears and laughter on seeing the return of a mother imagined to have been lost.

"If only you're right," murmured Ilario, "if only it's the way you say, and there is no such thing as evil."

"No personalized evil, at any rate; nothing with irrevocably evil intentions; simply one of the phases of becoming, a part of the practicalities."

There were several minutes now of vibrant silence in which the Count, who was no stranger to twinges of reverie, indistinctly sensed himself at the center of a triangle of attention that refused to reveal its major apex as lying within the room, and he felt his words to be surrounded by an obscurity compounded out of the attitudes they had excited: disconsolate admiration on the part of don Ilario; what he perceived as clearly an air of ingenuous amusement on the part of the Avaredos; and some anxious interrogation of which he intuited the presence without knowing from whom it came. He continued to hold his young friend by the hand, almost as though he himself, the carefree Lombard, were in search of a lifeline of solidarity.

"*O senhor* must be joking," Hipolito finally chimed with a vulgar grin. "No more than six years ago, *o demonio* appeared right here on this island—first in the form of a little bird, but then he changed himself into a snake, and later all sorts of other transformations. And he's still here now."

"Finally," chuckled Felipe, "he even asked for monthly wages and threatened to go to the independent trade unions; isn't that what they're called, *o senhor?*"

The quiet sarcasm of these jokes, so obviously aimed against a personage there is no need to name, suddenly had the power to make the Count blush; while encompassing how the Avaredo brothers' sense of realism was in its own way comforting, he nevertheless gave way to an anxious thought about the irreparable loneliness of the person it should most have been their duty to protect. He could see that Ilario was truly in the clutch of demons—far from material demons—that dragged him down into base, unnatural prostrations that might also contribute to explaining his incipient aging. And the Count, reacting to emergency as he always did, thought at once to make sail for safe harbor on the sturdy ship of practicality. The discussion had to find a mooring into something concrete, and he was at the point of asking the Marquis to give a description of whatever real work his philosophy of terror had inspired, or was about to inspire—still with the idea of proposing it to Adelchi Publishers—and in how many chapters of how many pages each . . . but the sensation of just a few minutes earlier, the feeling that his every word was the object of the febrile curiosity of a hidden ear, now crystallized into certainty. There was an eavesdropper! He had heard a pained sigh, almost the sob of a child in a fit of desperation, and now, from behind the edge of a curtain, he caught the sparkle of the eyes of the Iguana.

She had listened to everything! And she was avid, above all, for more, knowing herself to be the discussion's unnamed subject. Her eyes glowed with an attention so dark as to overwhelm all heed to the pack of books she clutched to her breast, and one of them tumbled down, smacking sharply against the floor, revealing her presence. The unhappy creature had no choice but to re-enter the room, pretending to have come directly back from her errand.

Full of a joy inexplicable even to himself and probably at variance with the sentiments of his hosts, the Count quickly stood up and walked in the creature's direction, just as he had done in the morning. He could hardly have acted otherwise. While removing the burden from her arms and retrieving the volume fallen to the floor, he managed to pass a furtive caress across her angular little brow as though trying to wipe away her fears. The beast made no reply, but once again tilted up her face towards the Lombard, studying him with soft, impassioned eyes that seemed a plea of infinite sadness: "Help me!" Then, she quietly left the room.

V

The Involuntary Indiscretion

A madman. Hypotheses.

A wind had risen, giving no sign it would quickly abate, though in fact it did, so rather than go out as usual to take their coffee beneath the oak tree, the Avaredos decided to do without it entirely and repair to their rooms for a brief early-afternoon nap. The Marquis, however, went to the kitchen and returned carrying a tray with a bowl of sugar, a pot of coffee, and two small cups (the Iguana seemed to have disappeared) and invited his guest to follow him to the library at the top of the tower.

Perhaps it was because the sky had slightly darkened, or because the quiet of the afternoon was absolute, without even the sound of the sea, but this room made no happy impression on the Count. It was tall, very tall and narrow with a vaulted ceiling, and its only opening was a single window set deeply into the wall, almost an embrasure. One could reach it by three slate steps, but it was sealed, rather than closed, by three leaded panes of stained glass. In front of it, at a slant, stood a school desk: the writing table of the man of letters.

The scant light that reached into the room after making its way up the stairs past a series of rigid portraits of absent-faced Portuguese kings was somehow cold and estranged from the world it found there. Invading that school-boy's desk, scattered with dusty papers and dry broken ink-wells and thus without a trace of any recent work, it seemed to whisper that nothing on these sheets of paper, absolutely nothing, would be worth being read, printed, or discussed. An alarming sensation. The light then rose to meet the room's rear wall and clambered up across the surface of a high oval painting, some two meters tall, where a woman about thirty years old—gentle, beautiful, and with a hint of the straight hair of the Marquis, of whom she was clearly the origin—carried some obscure, minuscule creature on her shoulder: it reached across a paw (its face couldn't be seen) to straighten a pale curl on her forehead. The mildness and spiritual grace of the lady's features, however, could not conceal that behind that forehead lay centuries of resolute will and command, of interest in the world, and simultaneously of implacable disgust in the face of its horrors—an array of feelings that might start to explain how an unsatisfied heart could seek refuge in what appeared to be a remarkably close relationship with a much-adored pet. Behind the woman's arm, which like the curve of her breast was veiled in blue tulle, one intuited more than actually saw a dark, greenish, foreign landscape that now—what with the paint's deterioration—revealed but a last few traces of glimmer on a lake in vague response to the final clearing of the sky after a day of storms and impetuous winds. Gilded letters beneath the painting spelled out the legend: I HAVE CHOSEN THE VOID, perhaps referring to a predilection for creatures that were mute rather than gifted with speech, or more simply to an inclination towards some mysticism for which the beautiful woman had suddenly developed a curiosity.

Noting the attention with which his new-found friend observed the portrait, don Ilario explained, after the appearance of a mild though fleeting smile in his eyes, that this woman, by now some years deceased, was his mother, a Hamilton, at the time when she and the former Marquis had lived in Tortuga, in the Antilles, where he too, don Ilario, had been born and had lived until he was thirteen years old. Six full years hadn't yet elapsed since he had come to join his brothers on Ocaña, and the monkey ("so it's a *monkey*," thought the Count, who had been convinced till then, though without knowing why, that it was some kind of bird), named Perdita, had been very dear to his parents and raised with him like a sister. At the time, they had kept the house full of animals, even dangerous animals, and whatever damage the creatures caused had always been tolerated with tenderness and infinite indulgence. He hadn't inherited the wealth of his parents (or rather of his mother, since the Segovias by that time were poor), but at least kept alive this cult of solitude where an infinitude of lessons can be learned by observing these sinless creatures called "animals" as they abandon themselves to thousands of extravagant games. Not all of them, of course, he added, are so innocent and trustworthy, but the majority . . .

After the experiences of these last few hours, the Count found this difficult to absorb. He felt embarrassed by what seemed to be a lie. But he also felt further warned about the lack of balance, even the delirium, of this young man's mind; he found it such a pity to watch the boy flail about in such obscurity . . . in what finally was a veritable triumph of ambiguity. The Lombard thus allowed his gaze to rove across the barren walls and to settle on the piles of books that had taken up residence on various monumental chairs or that lay on the floor in a disorder so great as to seem to give evidence of recent preparations for an entirely new order, if not even a flight (ridiculous thought) from the miserable island of Ocaña. His forehead was still slightly furrowed when his eye finally landed on a small yellow notebook, flanked by another that seemed more recent, each titled by hand in green ink:

35

first *Portugal*, and then *Penosa*, *"das o marques Ilario Jimenez di Segovia, conte di Guzman."*

"Are these yours? May I look at them?" asked the Count, instantly full of interest. Receiving a pallid smile as a sign of assent, he reached out to pick them up.

At times, you may have found yourself in similar circumstances; in the home of friends, perhaps, you may have obeyed the gesture of a distracted host and opened a door on a scene of great chagrin. Drawing back, for a person of any delicacy, is no more possible than continuing to advance, and the immediate reaction is the clammy sweat that breaks out on one's brow. Don Carlo Ludovico Aleardo di Grees didn't quite arrive at that—partly too because the Marquis' studio, exposed to the north, was fairly cold—but his soul, so to speak, closed up in a knot. He stared virtually in pain at that letter which served as a dedication to *Portugal*. Automatically and as though in a dream, he nonetheless began to read.

This, noble Reader, is the text:

> *Ocaña, the 37th day of October*
> *Present Century*

"Lodestar of my soul, dearest and most respectable *Senhora*, Perdita!

"On bended knee before Thee, I make bold to offer up in dedication this, my first poem!

"If all the constellations that are doubtless held upon the balustrade of the Universe by angels, archangels, and cherubim so that some pale light may come to fall upon our mystery; if, I say, all the best known constellations and others that shine no more, but that still are surely present, since time *o Senhora* is but a distance, and past and future reign

36

together o'er the impassioned and fulgent instant (if they do not likewise, as would be just surmise, wander as prisoners in the carriage of nothingness); I say if all these constellations, melancholies, and wisps of joy, along with those of other Universes, with all the silver fruits that multiply on the boughs of the Cosmic Tree (all places and events our base and sickly thought can barely sketch, never in any event, proceeding beyond the most risible suppositions); thus, if all these constellations, Milky Ways, these nebula, these contents, in short, of the night dispersed like oceans around our consciousness; if . . ." (and here came another twenty or more phrases, equally redundant, bombastic, and so extravagantly baroque that the Count found them utterly incomprehensible and therefore skipped them), "If," the writer again repeated, seeming finally to affect the form of a conclusion, "If they were all to think to burn together and thus to vanish into absolute infinity, they could not equal for an instant the fire that burns within my soul since when I have come, my Delight, to think on Thee as my wife and bride.

"Thou has deigned, bestial creature, to stoop low enough to reach me—bestial and thus the vehicle of all of Heaven's intentions and refinements. I then must make the effort to rise up to Thee. As a worthy son of Albion, I shall love Thee forever, o Senhora, and with devotion most impassioned. And though our sword have lost its ancient lustre, I, myself a descendent of the Hidalgos, shall place it at Thy feet. Thy name, in song that I shall sing, shall prick the jealousy of famous beauties, and armed with Thy name I shall sally forth into this age devoid of values to revive the spirit of those unfortunate men of genius who were destined so ill to be rewarded with worthless progeny. Thus am I charged, I, don Ilario Jimenez of the Marquis of Segovia, Count of Guzman, or who may hope to become such through the exercise of my virtues. Now, though, do not spurn me, nor leave me behind! Or know, if Thou doest, that swift death must follow on Thy sentence, in any case unswervingly just."

The words that followed compared this Perdita to a Spanish jasmine, or to the unquiet rosary of the sea on an April night, and the Marquis to a worm or a nullity if not to that other face, still in an unformed gassy state, of the Universe—which was the thought that gave a close to this incredible dedication, dated simply, as we have already seen, *"Present Century."*

Then, unfolded against the bottom of the page as though misplaced and forgotten, and supplying a contrast so dramatic that the Count at first did not grasp the entirety of its scope, there lay still another letter: a note from Lady Hamilton. It was a typically motherly note, pedestrian and heartfelt, to a forgetful son who needed to be reminded that she had had no word of him or her beloved Perdita since November, and please to remember that the *menina*'s food should consist of fruit and milk, several times a day, and a few well-roasted nuts would do no harm. She informed him that the Court in Caracas had decided against their "understandings." Even despite the Archbishop's intercession, not only the property in Tortuga, but even Ocaña, the last of the possessions of the Segovias, had to be considered lost. He was to ask Hipolito to put all the deeds in order, they were in the third drawer on the left of the wardrobe, because an agent from a real estate firm in Lisbon could be expected to come out to have a look around. Father, don Gonzalo, had suffered another attack of asthma, this time more serious, and fervently hoped, when this whole sad affair was over and done with, to be able to move to Havana, which was where they trusted soon again to embrace both him and his brothers. But no matter how things worked out, he was to continue to have faith in the Lord, since even though He seemed now to have chosen to allow the rise of the Hopins and to trample their own dignity underfoot, that didn't necessarily mean—and here she and the Archbishop were of the same opinion—that He intended forever to cancel them out of His memory. Then a verse from the Bible—a verse full of desperation, patience, resignation and hope—brought the humble letter to a close: "The Lord is the portion of mine inheritance and of my cup: thou maintainest my lot." But a few yellowing circles staining the sheet of paper were sufficient indication that the noblewoman, writing as she had, had said less than her melancholy would have prompted.

Even though the Count didn't have the kind of imagination that leaps and takes flight, quite the contrary, and even though he could never take an overview of the facts of a situation if not in numerical order (lacking, like many other Lombards, the gift of synthesis), he now—in fact for the very first time in his life—had the feeling he had understood much more than the jealous course of events had chosen to reveal. He connected the dedication and the accompanying letter he had found to the devastation of the house, the small island property, and now Ilario's studio; and he understood, or imagined to have understood, that everything he had thought till then about the Marquis, his brothers, and the cruelty of the lives they led, was no more than the fruit of a naiveté his own reductive mind hadn't yet outgrown. He might not be able to hazard anything about the brothers, since he couldn't yet say he really knew them, but if anyone anywhere in the world combined goodness and weakness, tenderness and misfortune, and all to the same frightening degree . . . well, that person now stood before him. If Ilario had gone mad, the reason could only be sought in the fragility and goodness, in the abundance of imagination and lack of practical experience that left him so exposed. It wasn't difficult to surmise, thought Daddo—while the Marquis busied himself beneath the desk picking up a few pen nibs that had fallen out of a box, thus giving vent to his desperation—it wasn't at all difficult to surmise, the parents having disappeared suddenly not only from Havana, if they got that far, but from the world in general perhaps in a highway accident or a plane crash or out of some adversity rooted in despair—no, it was far from difficult to surmise that the property in Tortuga had fallen into the hands of these Hopins, whereas Ocaña had remained unsold, or saddled with mortgages and other complications, or even perhaps saved *in extremis* through the archbishop mentioned in that letter; at the very least the Guzmans had been forced, if they wanted to maintain a hold on these few shoals, to make no further appearances on the mainland and to hope that Heaven had hidden their rocky fief from the researches of that real estate agent in Lisbon or touched the Hopins hearts to the point of making them forget about the place. The Marquis' madness had no doubt matured in this climate of fear and isolation even though its inception, as was clear from the letter, must have dated from earlier, from the time when he had begun to take the monkey entrusted him by his mother for some sublime little damsel. The monkey, by now, was most probably dead, or would have been sold by the Avaredos somewhere along the coast, and all that remained of the boy's fantastic infatuation was a vague, distracted sense of disgust for lower creatures in general—a disgust, unfortunately, now locating its principle object in the poor Iguana. Probably, as in the majority of such cases, the disturbance had started with the onset of the difficult age when boys develop into men, or into aspirants to manhood. It was a neurosis like any other, finally, and what was required to heal it was a real entrance into the world, the companionship of a friend, the attentions of women of feeling, and a mind-broadening participation in the discussion of certain political problems, not to mention a little money. Such things, and the Count had seen ample proof, could work miracles, so there was no reason to despair of subtracting Ilario from complete devastation. Careful to maintain his handsome face, both serious and smiling, in an attitude of respectful attention, he lifted his eyes from the page before him and directed them towards the Marquis, who squarely met him with his own gaze, but with unhealthily bright eyes. These pages, remarked the Count, seemed considerably interesting, and if it gave no offense he'd like to take the manuscripts back to his room. Then, making rather a show of wanting to look more carefully at this primitive, homemade edition of the poem, he once again leaned forward over the desk and was able to reach down to the place on the floor where he had seen a second copy of *Portugal*, undedicated. He quickly substituted it for the one he had first taken hold of. Ilario seemed so suddenly happy, so forgetful of his passions and so grateful for the Count's kind attentions, that Daddo's first misgivings, though not entirely vanquished, gave him peace and quietly disappeared. The two now began to talk about Milan and the possibility that works such as these (if Ilario were disposed for a moment to relinquish his position on the Universe) might encounter the favor of the greater public, which was always hungry for novelties, perhaps none too demanding, and therefore quite free with all its new money.

"I don't really know. . . . I'll leave it all up to you. . . . See what you can do. . . . In any case, I wrote these little works when I was still eleven years old, and I've never really gone back to finish them," said don Ilario, a trifle ashamed of his new frame of mind in light of the possibility of someone's making economic as well as social investment in his thoughts; and he wanted to entrust himself entirely to the discretion of his friend so that his own consent, which (he said) had mainly sentimental motivations, would give no rise to misunderstandings. He seemed almost surprised by his

own docility; and that dedication of October 37th, Present
Century, was suddenly nothing to be embarrassed about, nor
even, in fact, remembered.

VI

The Stones

By candle-light. Nature in alarm.

Night fell quickly after the Count retired to his room, and he was not at ease. One by one, he turned the pages of *Portugal* and *Penosa,* but he couldn't understand them and made the best of it by explaining his difficulties away. He ascribed the trouble to his limited knowledge of the language or to the room's scant light, since his friendly heart avoided admission that Ilario's inky world was only a tortured echo of greater, rightly-celebrated poetry on which the Marquis must have nourished himself ever since earliest childhood. Mingling with the exhausted blood that ran in his veins, it had filled his soul with that disconcerting spirit of rapture. He would talk about "adamite" sunsets, or abysmal caverns, or a battle betwixt two archangels, like furious cocks, within the shade of a cactus as the sun's first rays announced a new day. Or he saw damsels with peach-like cheeks and "diamantine" souls and clothed in raiments like clouds as they danced within the circumscription of a goblet. Or he would be hearing suavest voices and seeing green eyes as they rose from the depths of the Yucatan canal with invitations to a "paradise of tears" or some similar confusion. Maybe, after all, there was something good in it; finally it might be symbolism, with a mask no less sybilline than verbose denouncing the famous scourge of oppression. Anything was possible. Moreover, it was not for a Lombard Count to decide, nor for Adelchi, nor maybe even the critics: these two poems, exactly as they stood, perfectly incomprehensible, might have been purposely designed to excite precisely those feelings of perplexity and boredom that were a sure guarantee of good sales. (That goes to show you the character of our Daddo's mind; he was ignorant, or nearly, of the value of books, but that was usual in his century, and we won't rebuff him too severely.)

So his uneasiness as he lay on his bed had some other source, and he had no worries about his friend's health. Success and a modicum of money would quickly bring Ilario up to the best of form. What disturbed him had more to do with the cast of the sky, once again recharging, so to speak, with that sinister weight, that livid-gilt languor of the morning. The sea showed through the window's weathered frame as an enormous paving of crushed brown gravel with a great grey velvet drape hovering immobile along one side. The world lay wrapped in smokiness, the only real source of which was surely the fog now rising from the stand of oaks, if not the very temper of springtime weather. Everything was calm and silent, but touched with pathos, as though someone in a corner were repeatedly strumming a phrase of great sweetness on a ukelele. For a moment he also heard the thud of a hoe, wielded perhaps by the Avaredo brothers, intent upon garden work; then at once the nasal, worry-laden cry of a sea-bird made him start; and afterwards the silence hung so tangible as to urge his thoughts inevitably toward the frightened, infantile Iguana. Where, he asked himself, had the creature run off to hide? And in the wake of this question came a feeling that was not good, a feeling of some cruelty abroad in the world, some active opposition to goodness and happiness alive in the air and perceptible to Estrellita, despite her fathomless stupidity, as potential terror. Putting the poems aside, he sat up and looked around.

His room, like all the others, was very poorly furnished; one might even say a few dilapidated odds and ends contrived at concealing a total lack of furnishings. A sack of reeds, supported by two wooden planks on a roughly-hewn trellis, and covered by a threadbare blanket no longer white (absolving as well the functions of a sheet) served as his bed. There was also a rickety table, a wash basin, and an enormous closet. This closet now made the Count feel apprehensive, perhaps because one of its harp-shaped doors appeared to be ajar, which he didn't recall having noticed on first entering the room. Or had the muteness of the hour rendered all the objects around him strangely alive? His apprehension pulled him to his feet and made him walk over to the closet, opening it to see (nothing now would surprise him) if it might not contain some bird held trapped by a chain about its foot or maybe some small tiger intent upon combing its hair. But there was nothing of that, and the Count might have smiled if his heavy heart had permitted. There were only antiquated clothes and capes, slightly funereal bunchings of pink or green tulle, stuff that must have come from the Carribean, maybe Caracas, or Riohaca, or some place even further to the west, and . . . Here now was something he would not have imagined! Among all these old-fashioned clothes that rustled and gave off flashes of light like the feathers of birds was a thick wooden stick! Two! The summit of a ladder. Emerging from an open hatch!

After cautiously entering the closet, which was big enough, or deep enough, to contain a whole room, the Count peered down into the space below without catching the dimmest glimmer of light, and not even the faintest sound rose up to meet him. Remembering how his room lay directly behind the kitchen, on the other side of no more than a corridor, and that the kitchen surmounted the basement into which Estrellita had disappeared, he was amazed at architectural complications with which he himself, most certainly, would never have blemished his work. He had deduced that the servant's room continued beneath his own. Not that this really displeased him, but he felt irritation with the gothic and somewhat turbid mind of any builder who could contemplate a space in which a living creature, any living creature at all, was to be buried alive. Surely he had to be wrong. The likeliest thing, reconsidering, was for the room to have a few low basement windows, and the beast, exhausted by work or abundant tears, must have closed them, wanting to go to sleep.

A narrative account of these thoughts, by the nature of things, requires a certain arc of time, but they snapped through Aleardo with the speeds of dreaming, and descent of the ladder was already behind him. A flashlight brought from the *Luisa* in the morning sent a shaky beam of light before him . . . a beam of light that seemed to cower back, embarrassed, begging its proprietor for protection.

Never before had the Count seen such a pit, not even on inspections of the dreariest Milanese cellars. It was like a den dug out by foxes, and it finished in a sharply narrowing recess with a bed crumpled up at the very back of it, if the word can apply to a heap of filthy rags covered by a scrap of canvas. This was where the servant slept, in total darkness. A little to the front, where the room widened out, the corner of a case full of empty bottles contained a cardboard box with a few bandannas arranged quite neatly inside of it, including the scarf received as a gift from the Count. It lay wrapped in tissue paper along with a few colored stones. The care with which the scarf was folded, as though never again to be moved, spoke volumes to the Count, even though he saw no meaning in the stones beyond their preciousness to the little animal. As he trailed the white wing of his timid lamp once again around the room, still other objects, or symbols of objects, materialized out of the shadows: a newspaper, for example—spread on the ground and still fairly clean despite its quite remote date (headline news of a *revolucao* in Mexico)—served as a table and presented a well-ordered display: a shard of broken mirror, a fruitplate, chipped but clean and holding a few roasted seeds, and then . . . nothing more. But farther ahead, in a circular niche in the wall—perhaps a remnant of some ancient well—he saw a row of little packets of the kind that wrap coins at the cashiers' windows of banks. They were of all different sizes, no two alike, each tied shut with a piece of twine, and the Count was about to approach more closely in order to find out what they contained when a tiny noise from above advised him immediately to extinguish his light. With no suspicion of his presence, the beast was returning through the trap door in the kitchen floor. Soon he heard her footsteps, and even though he himself remained unseen, he could discern a few shadows in the greying beams of evening light now filtering down from the kitchen through the still-open hatch.

The Iguana was carrying a small shovel and a tiny pail, much as children play with at the beach, and without so much as removing the kerchief from her head she went straight to the recess where her packets were stored away. She opened one, as if checking that everything was in order, and the Count could see it was full of small stones, round, flat, all the same size. She looked at them, not avidly but somehow trying to form a thought of how best to protect and keep them stored in safety. They must have counted for her total riches. But she was likewise looking for something. . . . Then, having taken another scrap of paper and a piece of string from a hiding place, she tipped the pail over, causing a rush of still

47

more stones, these considerably larger; as she poured them out, her eyes cried drily, expressing a complaint all the more terrible for its utter silence. For a moment she stood simply looking at the pebbles, as though earthly riches no longer held any importance for her, and her little snout seemed changed into similar rock. Then she bent over and distractedly bundled the stones into a package that she tied together, up and down, right and left, dividing it into quadrants. She quickly scratched a hole in the ground and began carefully to hide everything away.

The Count had seen such operations in Milan too often to harbor any doubt about their meaning: these were packets of money. That's what the ill-starred servant had decided, or she accepted them as money because they had been given as such. Recalling Felipe's words at lunch about the servant's revindications, he realized that this was the coin in which her masters paid her. This was why the beast would have so bad a disposition and was always so nervous. But if she were aware that these stones were commercially worthless, thought the Count, why then would she treat them with such enormous care? He concluded she must have been entirely ignorant of the deception of which she was the dupe, and he considered it reprehensible on the part of the Guzmans. Yet poverty and need had been known to spawn even less pleasant subterfuges; and the Marquis, given his state of mind, was surely unaware of these transactions. Sooner or later, this was something they would have to discuss.

Now, in order not to frighten the creature, Daddo wanted to get himself out of this cellar, and the question was how to manage it. But other footsteps resounded unexpectedly from above, this time strong and human, and immediately afterwards a shout in the voice of Felipe:

"Iguana, where are you?"

And the Iguana's hasty reply, "I'm here *o senhor!* I'm

coming right away, *o senhor*."

"It's time to serve dinner; you should see it's already getting late. Then you go straight back to the chicken coop."

Felipe's footsteps soon walked sharply off, and the Count had only to wait until the Iguana, who for a moment showed no signs of life, should follow. Finally he could climb back up the ladder to his room. The sky had gone entirely grey, dawn-like, and the house appeared entirely lifeless. A moment later, someone knocked at his door, just as at lunchtime: the sign that the others awaited him in the dining room. He went to join them.

The table was set as at noon, but now bore two lit candles and a few of the bottles of Malaga the Count had brought from the *Luisa*. There was also a pie—Felipe's work again—concocted of boiled wheat, eggs, and a covering of crisp dough strips arranged into little crosses, each with a peppercorn at its center: to remind the assembled party of the mystery of the Passion and the Death of God. Instead of a first course of soup, there were onions and celery, dressed with vinegar.

The light was far from strong, but still quite lively despite the lack of draughts in the room (the air in fact seemed not to stir at all). Candlelight is always lively. Flickering across the faces of the Count's three hosts, its characteristic warm red glow showed him an apparent animation, no matter how slight, where in fact there was pure immobility. He had spent the afternoon in speechless sadness, and (absurd hypothesis) some secret circumstance might seem to have counselled that very same sadness to take leave of the souls of the Guzmans. The Count knew from experience that Hope takes not a single step unaccompanied by her sister, Sadness; and he argued that the latter, having called on him (she still remained by his side), had left the former to utter kind words to his hosts. And from affection for these unfortunates, he too was willing, he discovered, to converse with her. It was almost surprising. But after barely a moment, he realized that his curious state of mind reflected an underlying awareness of an injustice in supposing these people content with themselves in the treatment of their servant, and not simply forced to it by the gruesome poverty of their lives. Seeing that a strain of vitality now brightened their long thin faces and even lent them a renewed touch of youth, he returned more firmly to his first opinion that only indigence, and the pain that follows in its traces, could explain the harsh cruelty of their behavior towards the Iguana; he thus resolved to give fervent attention in the course of the evening to discovering a proposal that would put a redemptive end to a situation so thoroughly poisonous.

Meanwhile, the Count had noticed how the Avaredo brothers several times already had signalled some secret understanding back and forth between them with their sunken eyes; and he attributed it, perhaps, to some stupid appraisal of his clothing, which surely appeared bizarre, if not ridiculous, to these uncouth men. He didn't stop to think that any prerogative for such discrimination would have been far more his than theirs. Then, considering their repeated glancing at the ring he wore, as well as at his wristwatch sprinkled with small diamonds and crowned with a sapphire, he was momentarily shaken by an even more disturbing thought. Fortunately, he was able to dismiss it almost immediately: they asked whether his watch was running right, and could he please tell them the time.

"Eight o'clock," replied the Count.

At that, they exchanged a few words in such a harsh dialect of Portuguese that the Count caught only the phrase, spoken casually as of no particular importance, that by now *the tide was already high.*

50

The animation on the faces of the Avaredo brothers, though they added nothing more, then settled into a mien of more cordial tranquillity, an attitude of serenity that can even grace lugubrious souls when surroundings are utterly peaceful, as the island now was peaceful, except for, perhaps—it might have been only a sound in the Count's excited mind—a vague, intermittent squawking of the hens.

The Marquis' words, against this background, concerned the poems. He asked whether Count Aleardo had glanced at the works, what he thought of them, and whether they might truly prove to be of interest in Milan.

"Most certainly, my dear. From what I've been able to understand, your poetry connects directly to a painfully-felt tradition. Not exactly the going thing right now in cities like London or Milan, but connoisseurs, as always, are still to be found, people who can still appreciate a classical frame of mind. Even traditional works, if properly promoted, can do very well for themselves."

"But can an art exist," asked the Marquis, slightly hesitant, "outside of tradition? You seem to imply it can, if I understand you."

"You're quite correct," replied the Count. "There should really be no such thing, since art can only live within life itself, and life, when it isn't yesterday's tradition, is the tradition of tomorrow; but sometimes there's art without life, art without necessity. This is what happens when the wheels of the cultural industry turn entirely on their own."

"But to what possible end?" the Marquis rejoined.

For a moment the Count was nonplussed, thinking that a simple account of factual reality might disappoint the young man and further confirm his feeling that he was right to live in isolation. Any such risk, most absolutely, was to be avoided.

"In order," he therefore replied, "to encourage literary

production and enliven the movement of intelligent minds so that little by little they'll discover resolutions for innumerable spiritual and ideological conflicts."

"It's a question," countered the Marquis, after a thoughtful pause, "entirely a question, and I'm certain I'm right in saying so, of the love of life itself, and of hope. That's a wonderful thing, Daddo. So, in the kind of society you live in, young people don't find themselves isolated?"

"Not entirely."

"I've heard talk of realism. Maybe you can tell me what that means."

"What it ought to be," replied the Count, feeling slightly clumsy, "is an art of illuminating the real. But people, unfortunately, don't always affirm the awareness that reality exists on many levels, and that the whole of creation, once you analyze the deepest level of reality, isn't real at all, and simply the purest and profoundest imagination."

"I've had exactly that feeling, living here in my solitude," the young man exclaimed with an expression of joy that strangely affected the Count—an effect, though he understood the boy's emotion, almost of compassion. "You'll correct me, Daddo, if I'm wrong, but all of this could finally free us from the ancient conceptions of nature and spirit, and the real and the imaginary. That's what it all leads up to, now isn't it?"

"That's exactly it."

The Marquis exhaled a sigh, and continued, "There's no way I can describe the desperation of being alone; it carries you to the brink of madness. And all because your soul perceives the passage of time; somehow or another, it perceives the pendulum of eternity . . . but when you live in the islands, feelings like that get taken for silliness or some odd fixation. So in a way I've been right when I've imagined that nature isn't so impassive as some people" a clear reference to his brothers, "seem to believe. No, nature is not at peace She's like a mother whose son is in the grips of some calamity that's forcing him to abandon her . . . she's in a state of alarm, pressing her ear against every outcropping in the air. And so many strange sounds that we take for the creaking of a branch or the whisper of a leaf innocently falling onto a windowsill, well, they're really nothing other than her scratchings at the door of our cramped and contorted reasonings, her way of begging us not to abandon her . . . she'll find it terribly difficult to live without us."

Felipe had made a brusk movement in reaching for the wine, one of the two candles fell to the table and guttered out, and the Count saw none of the violent turmoil these words had brought to the faces of the people around him. The Marquis showed a flowering of pure love and terror; the brothers a form of dejection, almost a grimace of understanding. The Count only noticed, not without joy, that the ability to experience tender emotions, if only for a leaf or a tree, hadn't been expunged from the hearts of his hosts, or not irremediably and forever. Once again, as at lunch, he reached to his right and grasped the young man's hand.

"But nothing, my friend, can force us to abandon nature, which isn't really nature, or solely nature, but a part of us. Look at the bright side: she's fairly self-sufficient. God planned it that way when He created her, knowing perfectly well that humanity one day would abandon her and that she would have to live on alone."

And here, in support of his belief, he told the story of a rose bush he had once left, from simple carelessness, entirely without water in his house in Bellaggio; this thoughtlessness had later brought him to tears. But on his next return to his country house, he discovered that the rose bush, during his absence, had changed into a sunflower. Nature herself, in her infinite capacity for love, had seen to a metamorphosis, since it's common knowledge that the genus of the Composites, thank God, needs but very little water.

"You're a man of true goodness, Daddo," exclaimed the young Marquis, looking up at the Count from a face wet with tears yet lit in a radiant smile. "That's how things ought to be. As for me, I swear I'd go mad with joy if I could be certain that nature has no need of us."

Because the conversation, partly for these tears, was beginning to peak into moments of excessive urgency, the Marquis contrived to lapse to earth by explaining that his literary work, for some time now, had forced him somewhat to abandon his dear island of Ocaña to itself. It was blessed, in addition, by very little water, was battered by winds from every direction, and the sea, rarely so calm as during these last few days, was a frequent discouragement to the chores, repairs, and upkeep that needed to be taken care of, to make no mention of the island's being unequipped with agricultural machinery for rational exploitation of the fields; and frankly, he didn't feel he had the strength to join the labors of his brothers in trying to deal with such a predicament.

"If it's no more than that, my dear," assured the Count, first thanking Heaven for delaying any mention, till now, of a possible sale of Ocaña, "I'd be happy if you'd let me take personal care of the problem as soon as I get back to Milan. I'll ship you everything you need."

"You . . .you'd do that, Daddo?"

"If your brothers agree."

"*O senhor*, the Count, would be going to much too much trouble . . . it's really out of the question," said the two Avaredos with a single voice that failed, however, to tally with the sharpness of the look in their eyes. So far as the Marquis was concerned, joy and enchantment hung in momentary suspension on his face, and then once again withdrew like spring wings terrified by a sudden frost. His face again dissolved behind a gossamer of falseness that allowed only the passage of half-muttered phrases like:

"Thank you... thank you... but I really don't know... it's late now... very late, I'm afraid."

Owing in part to a returning surge, fairly distinct this time, of squawking sounds of hens, and also because the Avaredos, hearing this lament from their literary brother, dropped their faces into an expression of annoyance (reviving the barricaded atmosphere that had reigned in the early afternoon), the conversation grounded on an awkward silence. The Count, his open countenance likewise dimming, had ample time to reflect that he had certainly received no aid from a proper sense of delicacy and respect. The cruel *gaffe*, such as only Lombards manage to make, with all their forthright crassness, had wounded these islanders' flayed sensibility. Lowering his head, he strained to add, almost in a whisper:

"B..but, there's n..no reason to thank me... W..with your own w..works surely.... I had..d..hadn't thought..."

Stuttering occurred rarely in the Count's smooth, finely polished speech (it had been a frequent affliction during childhood), and together with a way his forehead would wrinkle slowly and his gaze go stiff, it was one of few signs that his soul felt cramped and distressed. This consternation only presented itself when he was certain, in the goodness of his heart, that he had harmed a living creature, regardless whether human or animal. His face would lose its felicity, and even the arid and heartless felt compelled to offer reassurance.

Don Ilario hastened to do just that, despite the bewilderment still coursing within his own breast.

"Listen to me, Daddo... it isn't pride that makes me refuse your help. If this land, after all, could be worked to yield a profit, I'd later be able to settle my debt . . . it's not pride at all."

"But why, then?"

"I'll explain," murmured Ilario, but he added no more. He regarded his friend intensely, as if seeing him for the very first time, and as he examined the Count he had the air of being none too present to himself, but the Lombard didn't notice.

"But the money . . . what would you do with the money you'll earn with your poems?" rejoined the Count, springing back to life in the midst of the decision that the boy's anti-quated writings must surely translate into money, as quickly as possible. Need be, and he himself would found a new publishing company as soon as he got back to Milan.

"It will not," he concluded, "be a trifling sum."

The Marquis' forehead crinkled again into a thoughtful frown. "You really mean that? . . . you're not simply trying to encourage me? . . . That's really true?"

"Absolutely. You can earn a great deal . . . I told you that before . . ."

Daddo was entirely unashamed of his words, since they were true, no matter how he had to make them true, and it would mean Ilario's rebirth and redemption.

"In that case . . . I'd give my earnings to the Cole Circus, in London." An astonishing reply!

With that calm indifference, that smile of complicity they typically assumed when taking charge of a subject first broached by their brother, the Avaredos explained that the Cole Circus had been dear to the late Marquesa. Now, how-ever, it was in steep decline—the spirit of the public having turned so grizzled on account of industry—and faced grave financial difficulties that could force it to strike its tents for-ever. The Marquis said nothing. But his face, as his brothers talked, veiled over with a sinister sweetness no different from

56

those clouds that end a day of uncertain weather by dropping unequivocally over the sun, restoring its tormented aspect, as least for the space of the coming sunset, to an appearance of renewed serenity. The Count, however—who knows why—had ceased to follow these infantile explanations, and his mind, as he knew it often to do, returned to an earlier point in the conversation. He remembered how at first Ilario had brightened on hearing the suggestion that a new agricultural flowering might be possible for the island; but he had immediately balked and refused all aid, bringing forth nothing but unconvincing doubts and hesitations. What could explain it?

"The Cole Circus. . . . But why the Cole Circus?" was all the Count muttered. Perhaps his voice went unheard; in any case he received no reply.

The Count felt thwarted by these new complications, which had once again reversed the situation and bathed it in the light of a desperation with no avenue of escape, or from which no escape was desired, and he momentarily gave in to the anxieties, maybe even the sense of hostility, that so lately had held his mind in sway during his visit to the cellars. Frankly, he felt forced to recognize that a nobleman's dignity, and even the faculty of poetic imagination, a kind of right to anguish, were one thing; and that the duty to provide for one's subalterns—especially children or animals, who are defenseless creatures of weakness entirely without resources—well, that was something else again. Quite involuntarily, in simple obedience to logic, his mind established the Marquis' negligence as entirely illicit even while his friendly heart, the Count's, was hastening to counsel itself to patience, supposing that the following morning would bring explanations capable of rehabilitating Ilario in his esteem. But this cost him no little effort and was made no easier by a growing sensation of sleepiness inspired by a rich and varied day.

The nighttime calm was interrupted once again by the noise of hens crying out like creatures molested by some intruding force, and the Count recalled that the Iguana, following Felipe's orders, should now find herself in the chicken coop. Though he had no way of knowing whether this was some nocturnal extension of her poorly-paid domestic services, or rather the terms of some incurred punishment, he concluded that the pitiful creature, like any other victim of oppression, was reacting by inflicting torment on others. He made a decision: no matter what it cost he'd ask the Marquis next morning to allow him to embark the little servant onto his yacht and back to Milan, where some religious institute could be entrusted with her education and where he himself might often visit her. During the voyage, and afterwards on Sundays in the visitors' room, he'd be able to question her, certain that the little Iguana's words would illuminate don Ilario's illness and indicate how it could best be cured.

Now, however, as Daddo shaped this thought, don Ilario newly fixed his guest with a sad and steady, dreamy gaze, remarking:

"If you're sleepy, Daddo, don't feel embarrassed to say so. All of us are ready for our rooms. The nights here are not short."

"*Porqué la lua está calando*," squeaked Hipolito's voice, but with a raillery that missed its mark since the Count was reabsorbed in his melancholy.

The Marquis too gave no acknowledgement to Hipolito's words, but reached across the table for the candle that had previously fallen and been relit. In silence— paying no notice to his brothers, whose eyes, sparkling in long thin faces, were as though magnetized towards the motions ensuing in now deeper shadows—he led his visitor to the door of the guest room and wished him goodnight. The two young men shook hands and exchanged a smile; but after closing the door of his room the Count knew very well that sleep, this night, would not come to join him.

VII
The Hat with Scarlet Feathers

A slow blush. To the hen house.

Alone now, the Count didn't bother to undress, but sat down on the bed, looking off in the dark (the Marquis had kept the candle) towards the open window.

Not since his time in Bellaggio, as a child in the house of a grandmother who enjoyed no fame for liberality in household expenses, had he ever again been in the dark, at night, in a room like this. Nothing about the poverty of the house left him with a particular taste of bitterness, but he was alive to an unaccustomed melancholy, most directly caused (he wanted to believe) by the powerful moonlight.

The whole universe seemed to be moving. The sky, scattered with oceanic wisps of brightness, almostas if streaming with scraps of tissue paper, was filling towards the horizon with a calm warm light. Surely that signalled the slow upward progress of the moon somewhere behind the summit of one of the island's hills, but it affected the Count like the bustle and vivacity of a house where a reception is underway; or where someone is in arrival, someone dear, and about to depart again. It's hard to say. Light was everywhere, but without being manifest; and liveliness and voices too, despite tender, unbroken silence. Daddo from his window then saw a stronger light in a hollow of the hill behind and flanking the house. Almost the red of a blazing fire, it confirmed his supposition that the aurora of the moon was now close by. The derision in Hipolito's words about the length of Ocaña's night, *"porqué la lua está calando,"* became quite plain, but the Count took no offense.

Why should the Marquis, if ever he found himself rich, want the Cole Circus in London to be his beneficiary when his own home housed a creature who received no reward for her services and was paid with pure stone?

Once again the Count suspected he might be making some mistake—a suspicion accompanied by a slow blush he perceived as a heat about his ears. He had the impression, the impression he invariably had when faced with some painful or difficult circumstance, that what most had gone wrong could only lie in some stiff recalcitrance of his mind, that his mind was incapable of grasping the reality of things. He felt mildly ashamed, and felt the shame grow sharper. That same mild shame, that vague lack of self-respect—as though ashamed of knowing his compassions to be worthless—had not infrequently caused him to lower his eyes as he strolled the world's paved streets. Hence his resolve to be more simple and active than he had been till now. He made up his mind to avoid these vague argumentations and to consecrate himself to offering real help.

"The little Iguana... must have a talk... make an offer... for everybody's good... a healthy sum... our liberation.... That first of all." The antique Lombard spoke to himself quite softly, pressing a finger to his forehead. He stood up and paced back and forth around the room, unaware of what he was doing.

Beyond the window, fairly illogically, was a small balcony. Illogical since it could only be reached by climbing over the windowsill, which the Count did instinctively. He was attracted by a high, rough parapet that would protect him, as it were, from the rays of the moon and their inviolate beauty, allowing him to remain hidden, as his soul desired, yet still a participant in the disarmed and disarming enchantments of the night; and after stretching out along the base of this wall, he discovered his concerns of barely moments before to have been displaced by an utterly different frame of mind: he could only think about his past, taking stock and passing himself in review. He seemed again to be a boy on some summer night in his native country province of Brianza, a beardless boy; and a familiar voice from someone bending over his ear, but whom he could not see, repeated an affectionate singsong: "Come on, Daddo, tell me where you've been, what you've done all these years, tell me about it." It insisted, mysteriously, "Something must be interesting in what you've done . . . come on, I'd really like to know. . . ." Without turning around, his reply maybe seeming a miserable admission to make, the Count pronounced, "Houses, *o senhor*, houses!" He heard a low laugh, and then bare feet walking away.

"Yes, I've done nothing but build buildings . . ." he thought. Nothing was wrong with that, nothing wrong at all, yet he looked back at his life and found it futile. As though looking at a void, an emptiness, a loss. As though considering a person who had known the benefit of large sums of money and had spent it on silly trinkets. On the other hand, that's what everybody did, and what was wrong with it? He would have liked to ask that voice what else he might have done, but his mind refused to couch so simple a question. He was now so devoid of all capacity for reaction, and so crushed, crushed to the thinness of a shadow by the secret of the world we inhabit—a secret grown painful, yet spiritually intact—that at first he paid slight attention to the light beginning to suffuse onto the balcony next to his own. The windows at its back swung open a few minutes later, and don Ilario stood outside, holding a small mirror in his hands.

The mirror was rectangular and framed in old gold, or bronze, something that gleamed, and this frame was sculpted with leaves. Surely it bore the remembrance of Lady Hamilton. Turned towards Aleardo, it allowed him a vision, an enchanted portrait, of the Marquis' face, which otherwise was hidden and could not have been seen directly. The Count had to admit it was a face of marvelous grace and luminosity. The lines and the worries that had caused them had been entirely cancelled out. Had simply vanished. Smooth as a cameo, but with accents of pink on its finely smoothed cheeks, that face spoke solely of the youth, the strength, and the glory of living in an eighteen-year-old body. The raggedy clothing had likewise disappeared, and the Marquis wore a hat of blue velvet, adorned with a cascade of scarlet feathers down to the side of his neck; a short, black satin cape covered his back but offered no hiding to a gloriously pied blouse: a thousand radiant colors over finely outlined shoulders, erect, elegant, and full of vigour. The rest of his clothing was black, and a low silver belt, chainlike, hung across his flanks and held up the grip, silver again, of a refined and elegant weapon. Like sapphires loosely fit into the alabaster of his face, his eyes shone brightly enough to be full of tears, but in fact overflowed with pride and joy. There was no longer so much as a trace of the devastations of aging.

In happy recognition of his own transformation, Ilario was giving the final touches to his hat with his perfect hand and leaned his head one way and the other like some exquisite bird of paradise. The Count observed this apparition with all the energy of his soul's distress, until pretended unawareness of his friend's festive air ceased any longer to be possible. He allowed his voice to reveal his presence.

"Slant it more to the right, my dear," (alluding to the hat) "so as to show your forehead."

Don Ilario did not respond immediately, as will happen

63

in dreams, where such moments may last even for two or three years. In the mirror, moreover, this image of great felicity seemed to waver and shudder. Then the boy complied.

"Are you going out?" the Count spoke again.

"Yes, I decided that taking a short turn couldn't do me any harm," he replied, "especially with the air so mild as it is tonight." But he advanced no explanation of his sumptuous transformation: neither of appearing in such refined clothing, nor of the youthfulness of his face. He only added, after a moment:

"Do you think there is anything—I mean something specific—that a lover could find offensive?"

"Nothing at all," replied the Count. "In fact, if the loved one sets a feather awry, the lover sees it as proof of the wrongness of everything that isn't set awry."

He laughed just barely, and don Ilario laughed as well.

"The same as everything else. Life itself surrounds us like a great dark sea, but can change its very substance," he remarked, "finally transmuting into quivering air. There's no other way to put it. And simply because our thoughts have caught a glimpse of the missing half that completes them, which can be monstrous or sublime; it makes no difference. Yes, Daddo, there's a truth in what you said, not far back, about the lack of any real division between the real and the unreal. Anything we even barely conceive of is immediately real. What we need: that's what's real! And we're ready to die for that, or sacrifice others. Neither our own death nor the death of others any longer makes a difference."

"Yes," concurred the Count, "that's how it is."

As he made this statement, he seemed to see a change in the color of the night. For a moment or so he paid the Marquis no more attention and let himself observe a more powerful brightness gulfing upwards and outwards until finding its way into the smallest clouds; millions of red birds might have been criss-crossing through the air. A clarity clearly red. The whole sky above Ocaña was turning red—but without any loss of its whitish, opalescent transparencies—as if due to a second moonrise. There were two possibilities, the Count thought weakly: either the first moon had been an appearance, conjured up from his own confusion and this new moon announced a return of faith and participation in the world; or Ocaña had two moons, which was truly absurd. No, now he was feeling better, everyone felt better, and that was all. His thoughts shifted to the mournful Estrellita. Why had the hens stopped cackling?

Steps sounded out in the room behind Ilario's balcony, and the Avaredos, as sumptuously dressed as their brother, soon appeared at the window.

"You'll be late," said Hipolito's voice, very softly, then adding, "Is *that character* asleep?"

"Indiscretion personified," from Felipe.

"Well, I can't really say he's wrong," admitted the Count after returning from yet another moment of faintness. "Nobody asked me to come to this island, but I came all the same; and now I see everything with startling clarity, even if the meanings of things remain obscure. Probably it's best to accept these visions. They apparently have something of which to accuse me. But I'll set out again tomorrow, and everything will be soon forgotten."

All the same, he was hurt that the boy didn't say good-by, leaving him feeling that these few brief exchanges had been dreamed.

The group had left the balcony, and the light of the candle withdrew from the room. The Count stood up, leaned out over the parapet, and looked at the black oaks, outlined in white; at the white sand, the dark sea. Then the beach showed the silhouettes, elegant and calm, of the figures from before. The handsome group reached the far end of the beach and disappeared, as though finding protection from the moonlight where the hill beside the house turned its calm bald forehead towards the cold winds from the north.

Ten minutes later—the time it took to stretch out once again, with the illusion of finding repose, and then to get up again, having seen that all such hopes were vain—the Count was convinced he must have dreamed. He had seen a young man who was the very image of happiness and glorious vitality, states for which Ilario (and this may explain why the Count had become immediately so fond of him) seemed not even to know the names. That shell of desperation, that froth on the surface of a nothingness or within a backwash of centuries of secret decomposition, had vanished and been replaced by an elegant youth with his mind in a fervent cloud of peace and playful fantasy: things conceded only by beatific innocence or extensive holdings of landed property; or, in short, by a conjunction of the graces of nature and economic clout. He was sorry to admit it (and also disturbed by his docile, impassive participation in that cruel conversation), but he was certain he had dreamed.

He closed his eyes, sighing, and then reopened them. It appeared that the sky had grown less red: the emotional convulsions of the universe might slowly be wearing themselves out and everything subsiding into approximate normality. Then the image of that small cortége, directed full of pomp towards the edge of the hill where the beach bent back behind it, returned to his mind with the precision of a photographic negative and such a grim charge of truth that he found himself whispering, "Where are they going...where have they gone?" He felt a nameless desolation. The care of Ilario's dress, his incongruous calm on being taken unawares, simply ignoring it, his brothers' sumptuous arrogance, the way they had all set off, so sure of themselves, down towards where the beach died out . . . all of it held something disquieting and pitiful, like a theater piece they were the first to recognize as fictive but that somehow, nonetheless, availed itself of his complicity. The idea burgeoning clearest was that the young man must suffer from an illness that the Avaredos, in the immensity of their common solitude, accepted and humored out of some sort of resignation. What else could they do on such an arid corner of the earth?

The Count was sadder and more awake than ever before in his life. On all sides, for as much as he could see of it beyond that wall, the island lay wrapped in a fog almost the color of copper: the combined effect of moonlight and low atmospheric pressure. It was stuffy, and the following morning would likely bring rain. There were no stars in the sky, only that indefinite, turbidly purplish luminosity that might have been compared—if women had ever been on the island, which was absurdly out of the question—to the ample unfolding of a ballroom gown the color of peonies. Within the glow, the Count discerned a point along the curve of the arid island's beach where the sea moved ever so slightly, as though half asleep. It made a low ecstatic sound as a paleness of foam at intervals appeared and immediately vanished. The Count could also see a few bushes in the moonlight, some glittering, others opaque. The *Luisa* too was visible, though running no lights. Salvato was surely asleep.

The Count had two valid reasons for feeling distressed (among others that were more ambiguous): the attitudes of Ilario and his brothers now stood clearly before his mind and were clearly unhealthy, and he had never ceased to feel great pity for the Iguana, who at this late hour was probably alone with her fears and painful anxieties. Something had to be done. No longer caring about being seen or heard by his hosts, who might return at any moment, the Count suddenly climbed over the parapet, slid down along the wall to the ground, and was standing in the open.

Moving away from the house, he immediately realized how rarely such a warm glow of light occurred in Milan, even during nights of July; and in any event, in Milan, it would have been due to the city's low position with respect to the horizon, certainly not the case on Ocaña. It was this light, surely, that had created so many curious enchantments and had led him even to maintain that love and murder might be compatible. In reality, he had always felt that love's truest and inevitable function was the resurrection of the dead. But with that brief exchange of words on the balcony, he had begun to live in a state of hypnosis so strong as to leave him incapable even of noticing sensations or suspicions which at any other time would have struck him as odd and induced him to seek out their causes. Things would hopefully settle into more proper proportion in the morning, or after a good sleep. Right now (this thought was fortunately clear) his task was to find that chicken coop where the Iguana was locked up. He'd be careful not to frighten her, but he had to ask the creature for whatever information she could give about the Marquis' illness, or about its first visible symptoms, and whether, as he sometimes suspected, the poor man's infirmity hadn't made him the victim of some base machination on the part of his brothers. Finally, too, he wanted to ask Estrellita if aside from housework there was anything she knew how to do . . . if she had ever gone to school. Such an absurd hypothesis! But it was part of his way of taking an interest in such an unfortunate life, and part also of a somewhat painful admission that the Lombard capital doesn't offer the same sympathies and advancements to rudimental beings as to descendants of highly placed families. The Count wanted only the best for his protégée. No matter how things stood, he would negotiate pre-emption on the very next day, and he had no doubt that a sufficiently high figure would bend the Guzmans to acquiescence.

These were his thoughts as he started off towards the hill through that scalded air. He was far from happy, however, even though faith and his inborn goodness had not abandoned him. He continually told himself that the solution to the problem was easy; but he also felt, simultaneously, that the Iguana's liberation was a difficult goal to accomplish, entirely impossible. This sensation, though he strained to shake it off, made him move about in search of the beast much as in former times he had piously approached the mossy stone covering the grave of a forefather, servant, or much-loved friend, whom no act of piety could reawaken.

VIII
Daddo Disturbed

I saw you making piles of coins. The beast dreams.

The shack where the chickens were kept, and where the Iguana too seemed sometimes to pass a night, was not very far from the hollow planted with olive trees where the Count, in the morning, had helped the poor unfortunate pull a bucket of water up out of the well. He approached it, and even though the copious moonlight was deflected here and there into shadows thrown by the olive trees, he had a perfectly clear vision of the enclosure. Part of it, towards the back, was protected by a canvas intended to ensure the sleep of the fowl, but the front stood open, open now to the moonlight. And here was the Iguana, absorbed in an occupation that had the force of a sudden truth—one of those truths that can enter our vision with instant clarification of some previously ambiguous or at any rate uncomfortable situation which we've taken from time to time as a source of worry and affliction. The mind of our tender-hearted visitor experienced the sudden collapse of every suspicion of evil, and almost of every reason for pain.

The young Estrellita (for no further doubt remained about her youth, even her callow infancy) had drawn a figure on the ground with a pointed stone, and this figure was that very same rectangular enclosure that you yourself will so often have seen children make, and with which you too,

Reader, as a child, will sometimes have whiled away the hours. Such an enclosure is internally divided into six sub-squares plus a seventh at its summit, this seventh in the form of a semi-circle; and the game, which consists of throwing a pebble into the grid and then skipping on a single foot from one square to the other without stepping on any of the dividing lines, is known not only as "hop-scotch" but also as "the days of the week." An ingenuous game, and a thousand times more ingenuous, if not downright bizarre, when played at night by a creature like the Iguana, whom once already the Count had observed as she suffered and sighed while counting money in tremendous silence and with all of an adult's sense of suffocation. Practically as though the night had freed her from the presence of the atrocious beings surrounding her, and had somehow reawakened her to an atavic stock of happiness, the Iguana was making little jumps and passing lightly from one square to the other. A few hens, awake and offended, watched her from their perches; the Iguana, just as children anywhere in the world would do, appeared to pay them no attention. When she turned her thin snout towards the Count, the young nobleman recognized that the course of her daily life had, yes, left wrinkles of terror and anxiety on her face. But he also discerned an indefinable light of grace and joy, and it didn't extinguish when he lit his pipe and approached the chicken coop, the smile on his face both timid and pleasant.

"So that's why the chickens weren't asleep," he graciously remarked. Yet he was thinking about how she would look, washed up and put properly into order, on being taken to school. Among thousands of other little girls she would cut as pretty a figure as any.

The Iguana laughed, and one might have believed her tiny soul truly to have been healed and liberated from every bitter shadow of fear; or at least she appeared to the Count to be laughing. He had discovered two small teeth in her face—two teeth, moreover, spaced at considerable distance from one another. But she was by no means homely. To the Count she seemed so pretty as nearly to leave him convinced he had always been aware of it. He even had the impression her eyes weren't really all that small; that they were in fact quite large and splendid; calm more than anything else; they might, like a well, reflect the entire disc of the moon. This impression, however, did not last long. The Iguana abandoned her game, came up to the fence to stick out her snout between two staves, and her eyes were once again small and serious. They seemed to the Count to be full of gravity and allowed him to speculate that the Marquis' madness had not much spared that tender mind. She looked at him, yet not with the aura of a little beast, or a young Iguana. . . . Not even the Count could have said how she looked at him, but those eyes contained a severity and a lacerated, interrogative air that ranged far beyond the limits of their conversation, which developed like this:

IG.: "Don't you feel like sleeping, *o senhor?*"

COUNT: "No, Estrellita. . . . It appears that you don't feel like sleeping either. . . . What game were you playing?"

IG.: *"La semana, o senhor."*

COUNT: "Is that a game you can play all alone?"

IG.: "Yes, *o senhor.*"

The Count propped an arm against the hen house roof, and while looking down at this extravagant little creature he discovered her bright, steady eyes to hold a suaveness he had never seen in anyone's eyes in Milan. They filled him with a calm, grave sense of the secret of the Universe, of all the abysses surrounding us, and of their highly probable goodness. He was no longer troubled (who knows how or why?) by all the oddities and stiffness of his hosts, not even by their excursion out beyond the hill. While feeling so perfectly serene, he was also a little heartsick; conceivably he was guilty of something, but he didn't know what. Surely the answer had to reside in that miserable green little figure illuminated by the light of the moon.

"Listen, Estrellita, there's something I'd like to say to you," he continued after a while. "Do you mind if I call you Estrellita?"

"No, *o senhor.* . . . What is it, *o senhor?*"

He had been right to expect a reaction of alarm.

The girl-beast's eyes showed a sudden disquiet, the Count's mild worries having possibly bridged across from himself to her. Diverting her gaze, she repeated:

"What . . . what is it?"

"I saw you making piles of coins," the Count unexpectedly rejoined. "At your age, you know, that's not a good thing to do. I saw you in your room . . . looking down through the trap door."

This was not at all what he had wanted to say. But perhaps he spoke these words since only a reproof—cruel for utter lack of justification—could have expressed the pained, delicate emotions intertwining their fingers in his head. He could find no way even to feel ashamed, nor to comprehend what truly was wrong with him. So he looked at the Iguana with still greater severity.

"But that wasn't money, *o senhor!*" replied the little servant, staring at the Count with suddenly hard eyes after a short span of surprise.

"Ah! That wasn't money! So what was it then?"

"They were stones."

The creature's tiny eyes shone with a moment of heavy darkness that wounded Aleardo, but then grew softer, little by little, until turning finally into what the Count would have described as an attitude of timid surrender. She eventually admitted:

"Those were my savings, *o senhor!*"

"But why do you bury them?"

"I don't know. That's just what I do."

This explanation, given hastily with the same hard tone, also bore a touch of cunning: comfortable in her own few inches, the Iguana might have been measuring the ingenuousness of the towering Lombard noble. Yet her mood didn't hold. Clouding curiously over, she receded once again into will-less acquiescence and confessed the misgiving that Felipe and Hipolito might come while she was away and reclaim the "money" since they had never been happy about letting her have it.

"So, before they didn't pay you at all?" asked Aleardo. Her little hand lay in his line of sight and he observed its dirty fingernails.

"They gave me other things, *o senhor.*"

"And what would these other things have been?"

No reply. What was the Count to argue to himself except that she had lied once again?

He reconsidered, however, when he took that filthy little hand into his own and found it so amazingly cold and inert. Perhaps she had offered him less a lie than an image. A connection coalesced between the darkness of the atmosphere, the creature's amazement, and how "other things" had been spoken so quickly. Why not imagine that "other things" might be consubstantial with affection, humanity, and gracious expressions of kindness? And now they were over and done with, conceivably because of some grave incident, or some mutation in these people's lives. Or not a mutation, but simple upcreeping indifference, as can happen so easily in the course of relationships. Afterwards they decided to pay her, offering an order of material values as assuagement for distance and suffering. Yet that wasn't quite right either. It seemed the Iguana herself had demanded a regular exchange of money in absence of friendlier arrangements, if the word "money" could apply to these ugly stones.

"I think you must be very fond of the Marquis," he said, ending the pause. Then he lifted his eyes to look at her and found himself wondering about the nature of the abyss into which the Iguana had retreated so successfully for refuge on hearing these words. It was nearly impossible to make her out. But this was the fault of a cloud that had drifted in front of the moon, though partly too because the Count's memory had momentarily failed him. It was clear to him now that the Iguana did not at all like this conversation; and, to tell the truth, that he didn't like it either. Tears almost came to his eyes, and his mind inexplicably moved back to the thought of how his life had always been so much akin to a great long sleep: "Houses, *o senhor*, houses." There were so many things no longer to care about, and somehow he allowed his unfortunate question to drop into a void. His expression shifted in a way a sensitive friend would have noticed, but hardly a downcast, extravagant young Iguana, and he continued, quite simply, yet at enormous expense of will power:

"Then why are you going away?"

"But I'm not going away, *o senhor*."

"And . . . would you like to go away?"

"No, no!" the creature replied, really more with a movement of her head than with her voice, which had faded to little more than a rustle.

"My dear little Iguana . . . I want you to listen to me . . ." began the Count, before finding he could go no further.

Meanwhile came the thought, "She's really very beautiful." You might have said him incapable of making any appeal to reason. "I can't understand how the Marquis hasn't fallen in love with her. . . . Maybe it's because she has no

75

soul." His tears now rose relentlessly.

"Didn't you want . . . to say something to me, *o sen-hor?*" asked the Iguana.

"Yes, Estrellita, I do. Have you ever been married?"

"No, *o senhor.*"

"But wouldn't you like to dress up in a lovely veil . . . and come away to Europe?"

At first the creature just stared at him, and then began to laugh with the silent embarrassed laughter of children. But she was serious again as she curtly replied:

"No, *o senhor.*"

"But why?" asked the Count, his question virtually a lament.

"Because I wouldn't."

"That's no reply at all," he thought. Then he also thought, "But I don't really feel well. Here I am in the middle of the night on a desert island called Ocaña, walking up to a chicken coop and asking a tribulated young Iguana whether she'd like to get married and come with me to Europe. She's still too young for any interest in a thing like that, and I've forgotten my own intentions. I've been thinking all along of my duty to assume the role of a father in her life. The world contains quite enough husbands already. Even too many, and no fathers at all, as far as I've been able to tell. There's an obstacle remaining in this case too: is it possible in fact for an immortal spirit to make itself understood in a dialog with irrational Nature? And what is it, this thing I'm calling Nature? Is it good or evil? What are its needs and demands and expectations? It's clear that Nature suffers . . . and requires our help. But can such a thing be possible without risking eternal death?"

That's how the Count was thinking, aware too of a chill. Releasing his gaze from the Iguana, who silently continued to stare at him, he turned and walked away. What he felt was less humiliation than sadness, a feeling of being at loss, such as only simple men experience when abandoned by God-given peace of mind.

IX
Ocaña's Two Moons

Another boat. Surprise!

The Count made off towards the house, but chose the longer way around, for simple lack of courage. That dreary dwelling was no place to go in immediate search, let alone of relief, but even of the meagerest refuge, some repair against vague melancholy and besieging thought. Rather than sentimental, his dilemma now loomed up as virtually theological. His route, as you'll understand from the drawing, took him to the east, considering the island's conformation in a half-moon shape with its hump towards the coast of Portugal:

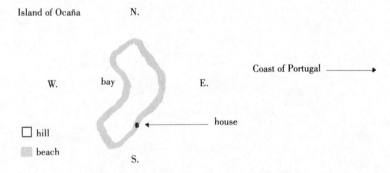

Island of Ocaña   N.

W.   bay   E.   Coast of Portugal ⟶

☐ hill

▨ beach   S.

house ⟵

Turning northwards across the hill that hid the island's natural inlet, the path then doubled back and finally met the small southwest beach where the Count's hosts, dressed fit for a gala reception, had slipped out of view an hour or so before. Feeling disturbed we often desire to dawdle, and the Count envisioned the difficulties or curiosities of the longer path as a possible distraction from his light but mortal sadness. Presuming that the dawn, as usual, would settle his thoughts and point out his simplest obligations, he instinctively attempted to avoid all struggle with his intricate problem until sunrise. Reaching the summit of the hill, he turned to look in contemplation on the mysterious west—he hadn't had a glance in that direction for the last few hours—and his reasons for wandering brought him face to face with what he had taken for an entirely imaginary moon; slow to plumb the gravity of so bizarre an occurrence, he at first admired it with a sense of pleasant surprise.

The first moon, orangish and slightly prolonged like the yolk of an egg with an image of a chick inside it, was already rising, possibly struggling, up from behind the promontory and was beginning to pale; and the Count now recognized the second moon, in all its unnatural vivacity, as the lantern of a ship. It was a vessel, moreover, that deserved his whole attention: a dark, three-masted boat standing motionless at anchor in the harbor, entirely alone like some lost aquatic bird. Unmistakably powered by sail and of far from modest proportions, it was much more likely a merchant ship than any sort of pleasure craft. Its darkened portholes gave no sign of life aboard, and this great marine creature might have been attracted to Ocaña by a dream rather than intentionally piloted to port on a specific mission. Then, as the beacon turned before blinking out (so someone surely had to be aboard), it threw its full illumination on a row of boxes and barrels piled up along the shore. The glare drew them up closer to the Count in the most extraordinary way, and they seemed to have been just unloaded or about to be embarked for definitive departure.

Aleardo was astonished, and alerted all his simple native goodness into calling himself back to order. There was no need for fantasies that might lead to any ulterior infringement on proper discretion and to an unallowable, uncalled-for curiosity about the island's secret life. He knew his obligations and passed but a very few instants in meditation of the scene. In fact, he was already turning his back to it when his eye caught the appearance, down where the beach rounded back into view after skirting the promontory, of a short procession headed, this much was certain, by the Marquis' brothers. Following came don Ilario himself, his arm extended to a person of the female gender. Another individual, again of that gender, but extraordinarily tall and lanky, tarried a little further back on the arm of a being precisely her opposite: short, broad, and defined as male by the shine of his scalp in the moonlight. Concerning three other persons there was no possible indecision: a prelate, an altar boy, and a Negro maid in a lavishly flowered dress.

Happy that his perplexity about the mysterious sailing ship had been so unexpectedly dissipated, and happier still that don Ilario's solitude was not to be classed as irremediable (really, to be precise, the solitude of Jeronimo Mendes, since this, with an inexplicability we won't attempt to tamper with, had suddenly disclosed itself to the Count as Ilario's *inner* name), Aleardo was now disturbed solely by the realization of his clumsiness. He had been so maladroit as not to understand, during dinner, that the Guzmans were preparing for visitors, and he had stumbled here into a truly indelicate situation. He decided on a rapid return to the house so as to re-enter his room before the procession should reach the clearing with the oaks. He would immediately go to bed and fall asleep, and he would be ready at earliest dawn to return to the *Luisa*. The Iguana remained an ever-present clutch in his chest, but for the moment he didn't want to think about her. He may even have been grateful for the chance development that constrained him to set the strange question aside for a while. Because the human heart, even the heart of a Lombard Count, at least within its less enlightened folds, never loses the occasion to defer fulfilling a duty that threatens to tax the spirit with problems and complications. It may not always seem so, but there's a fundamental laziness in the human heart.

Minutes later he had to choose between two admissions, both disturbing: that the beach, for example might be connected to the house by a subterranean passage; or that his curious hosts, like witches, were less in the habit of walking than flying. Nearing the house he realized that the Guzmans as well as the others had managed to arrive before him, as was really quite obvious from how the windows, thrown wide open to the night, emanated a uniform reddish light mixed with dense billows of smoke smelling of nard and incense; and even more than visible, it was audible from a high, impassioned sound of religious hymns, accompanied by low litanies and the rumble of an harmonium, all of which waned and came to a finish, as though by chance, when the Count was only a few steps away from the house.

If, from the top of the hill, Aleardo hadn't already seen the short procession with its rear brought up by the prelate and the altar boy, this new surprise might have troubled his imagination; but having seen these religious images, he could combine them with these clearly religious odors and sounds and know why the house had been illuminated into such a fascinating presence—fascinating at much the same time that another part of his mind, experiencing a twinge of bitterness, shied away from the moralistic violence of an apparatus in which the Divine Spirit could so deliberately face off against evil, treating it like an adversary and intending to force its dark forehead forever downwards into the shades.

Uneasy, indeed somewhat annoyed with this reappearance, even here in the midst of the watery ocean, of an authoritarian Church with an implicitly politicizing manner of addressing the abyss (calling it polemics still put it too lightly), the Count resolved to have nothing more to do with it. He would seal off his eyes and ears, since the illness of the young Segovia-Mendes was beginning to depress him. And illness, surely, was how he'd refer to such a discouraging obsession. The Marquis seemed happy, moreover, in the company of minds no more open than his own.

The Count was now on the left side of the house, having carefully circled its facade, and here, where there were neither windows nor doors nor other openings, he felt slightly more at ease. But he couldn't relax entirely until reaching the back of the house where he saw an open kitchen door, an entirely empty kitchen, and clear passage to the cellar hatch. He wished to pass entirely unseen, sparing all new embarrassment to his hosts; so he would reach his own room by way of the Iguana's underground cell. In doing so, or rather while making his way to the small trap door, he brushed against the vast kitchen table and discovered it decked, to his enormous surprise, with all of his bottles of Malaga, not a few bottles of sparkling French wine as well, and then glasses and a soup tureen brimming with crisply fried fritters sweetened with honey, most certainly the work of Felipe. Fritters in a wash of light from the now pale moon that shone through the rickety door.

"So . . . after the benediction, we also get a reception! . . ." he said to himself, charging his exclamation with an edge of scorn for which you'll see no need to hold him responsible. It was only a passing emotion, and he had, after all, been left uninvited to the feast. There were ways and times in which the Count still reacted like a boy: further revelation of a thoroughly artless soul. Afterwards, moreover, a truer displeasure hastened into his thoughts, truer if only because he could admit it quite openly: what about the Iguana? No sweets, no toasts, no reception for her. They appeared to have gone so far as to turn her out of the house to prevent her from stealing a look.

Felipe's words, *"Then you go straight back to the chicken coop"* quickly returned to his mind and linked with the chain of all these new and unexpected circumstances. They began to throw a light, though slowly, upon a situation quite suddenly perceived as densely, particularly suspect. If the little servant, as one would presume from the ease and lack of resistance with which she took such orders, was banished every night from the house, such a thing must mean that this scene of disembarkation, with the house then visited by strangers, was likewise a nightly occurrence, or had been for at least the past few days. Perhaps the house received a benediction every night. The packing cases on the beach made a clear announcement: someone was about to depart, and someone else to arrive in substitution of the former proprietors. A substitution that might be entire and definitive displacement. Still other words spoken at dinner came back to mind. The Count had been quite startled by don Jeronimo-Ilario's *"by now it's late, very late, I'm afraid,"* but the phrase now aroused an unexpected compassion for the sad young man and stabbed the Lombard noble with a moment of pique for having behaved with such silliness. He could be certain that the house, if not the island itself, was up for sale: Ocaña was about to receive new masters and such a change might offer sufficient explanation for the generally desperate atmosphere, and for the fear coursing through the beast. All of it entered him like the slowly mounting light of a coming day— a startling clarity that could only continue to grow and never possibly diminish, while nonetheless remaining an absolute mystery.

Not even the memory of the Marquis' transformation

while standing on the balcony and making repartee on the sublimity of love, not even this was enough to attenuate it. Quite the contrary. The Count's increasing doubt about the Marquis' peace of mind derived precisely from these words and the arrogance with which the boy had spoken them. They surrounded too with an ever sharper melancholy as the Count reflected on his own unconsidered acquiescence. Then, in this split second, whether or not the moon had disappeared, the kitchen doorway began to grow dark, and this sudden revelation of the blackness of the night appeared to give new urgency to the pain the Count had felt during his dialog with the Iguana—a pain like an intuition of a supreme and fundamental inability to grasp some truth similar in every way to the light of that moon: an absolute presence, yet perfectly concealed.

X

A Family of the Universal Type

The archbishop.

Darkness, we remarked, enveloped that door previously whitened by Ocaña's first moon, and the Count descended through the hatchway. Still absorbed in his sullen thoughts, he had barely pulled the trap door shut behind him when footsteps and excited, somehow imperious voices sounded out from directly above. The new arrivals had reached the kitchen. At this point Aleardo would have liked to turn back: that he ought to present himself to the company any man of his caste would find natural; he himself, a short time earlier, would have known no hesitation. Now, however, he was stymied by a numbness he had never before experienced, a mood of chilled sadness at odds with both his breeding and his inborn generosity.

Just as a boy wrongly rebuffed by his mother will tarry listlessly in a corner, the Count gained the secret passage beyond the second trap door but didn't immediately abandon it to re-enter his room; he remained, instead, inside the closet, waiting for sounds or sights that might rise from below. Meanwhile, though no more openly than with a twinge just slightly stronger than a normal beat of the heart, his determination to foster some course of action for the salvation of Ocaña and its variously desperate inhabitants proved itself more dormant than defunct. It stirred again in his mind, and his plan to depart from the island at dawn might never have existed.

After only a few moments the Count's hesitation was amply rewarded. The trap door from the kitchen lifted open (as was plainly visible from the closet) and flooded that savage subterranean fastness with a wide red shaft of light while several individuals began to descend the stairs. They were clearly the people he had spied out on the beach. Felipe preceded them with a torch in a globe of vermilion glass.

You'll see now that the secret of things is often much more modest than infantile imaginings on the nature of the Universe obtain a more or less inexplicable pleasure in attempting to demonstrate. These people were simply the members of an orderly, very proper little family of the worldwide middle class, which is the American middle class since all little families everywhere are today American, and the Yankee origins of this one were particularly clear. They were a wide father, a long mother, and a very resolute daughter between twenty and twenty-two years old with a thin face, black eyes, sun-tanned cheeks in gay contrast to a bright red cocktail dress, and a nose of the slenderest, most decided interventionist grace to be found on the earth's many continents. Indisputably a queen of hearts and fortunes, this fine young woman now, however, advanced into this dismal hole with just the proper hint of conventional alarm and no more than the proper minimum of true attention—dosages sufficient to show that her sporty soul was not entirely indifferent to the fascinations of the horrid or to the magnetism of natural depravities (natural where indigence ran to extremes). By way of contrast, the mother's misgivings were more open, possibly indicative of real bewilderment; but the woman herself, attired in caramel-colored chiffon, various gold and silver trinkets, scraps of lace and sprays of feathers, was no less than a fountain of light. She glittered from the tips of her moon-hued sandals to the copious brim of her dawn-pink hat (a veritable allegory of summertime with poppies and sprigs of wheat blown awry by invisible winds), from the silver of her fingernails to the treble bags of mauve that rose beneath her eyes to hold the rims of their lower lids aloft and fully in view. Mister husband and father, the master of some farm in the backlands of a western metropolis out where the forests begin, was in no lesser form, even if attenuated, perhaps almost dominated, by an attitude of vigilant prudence. Swathed in raw silk and gold, and carrying a bamboo cane, he seemed at every moment to be exploring the poisoned basement air, searching for just the right path where his ladies might advance without the risk of some sudden interference from unexpected obstacles. A perfectly superfluous precaution: to the eye of the Count's Lombard mind, the Iguana's home stood more inanimate and prone than at any time before—something on the order of a tomb from which the creature had been evicted by warrant of a supernatural division of police. The servant's dwelling was now no more than a storage place for wine in tall casks, or casks lacking wine, and boxes crammed with disparate odds and ends. The corner where with her smallgreen hands the child-beast had buried her treasure of stones appeared so unprotected and so openly proffered to the torchlight that the Count—despite the reaction's senselessness—began to tremble, expecting its imminent discovery.

This was hardly likely: the successive appearance of still other visitors was soon to fill the room with a delicious vivacity. Hipolito and the distracted Marquis were just a few steps behind.

Don Fidenzio Aureliano Bosio, a characteristically Lombard face and currently Archbishop of Merida at a distance of seven hundred kilometers from Caracas, was a person with whom the kindly Count was by no means unacquainted. Aleardo's features afforded this sole conclusion, opening into a smile at the very first sight of him. This courteous self-satisfied figure, infinitely rosy, red, green, and golden within the wonderful stole that covered his shoulders, was nothing less than a protégé of that same maternal grandmother whose home in Bellaggio had been the scene of Aleardo's childhood. Having first discovered the charm and persuasion of Fidenzio's voice and then the poverty of his origins (he lived in a ramshackle farm house along with a dozen brothers and looked forward to no discernible future), Grandmother had in fact adopted him, true to the violence Lombards typically employ in doing good works. The expenses of his seminary studies had been defrayed by a not inconsiderable portion of the funds she regularly earmarked to "charity." So Aleardo had met the promising student and future theologian on any number of occasions in the garden and downstairs drawing room of the villa: occasions when golden liqueurs and crisp pastries unfailingly emerged from heavy walnut sideboards and flower-encrusted porcelain boxes. Whenever she looked at him, Grandmother appeared to rediscover the peace of mind that a pursuit of romantic ideals from the time of her maidenhood had seemed to endanger, and don Fidenzio, though counselled to caution by an erudite scruple, had given her the most formal of assurances on the final salvation of her soul. The gentlewoman's beauty was still quite remarkable, no matter that her greenest years were long since gone, and Fidenzio's guarantee allowed her to concede herself a few more generous follies, after which the officials of God had fetched her away. At that final juncture Aleardo had been about twenty years old, and his almost-brother, just recently consecrated to the service of the Lord and about to depart for the Balearic islands, was close to twenty-five. Aleardo had watched him stroll the garden

promenade overlooking the lake, and since that day ten sum-
mers had passed with no additional news until this evening's
sudden and highly pleasant surprise.

What a wonderful prospect. He could renew a friendship that also promised the blessing of a solemn clarification
of the mystery of Ocaña. His spirits changed so utterly that
he had to restrain the joyful urge to reveal himself and rush
immediately out to embrace Fidenzio. But as morning would
be time enough for the revelations he so ardently desired, the
Count now prepared to retire from the closet and put an end
to this curious evening. What made him falter was the vision
of what the prelate, followed by Felipe and the altar boy, now
commenced to do: they were making the circuit of the cellar,
Felipe shining light into all its corners, the altar boy waving
his censer, the thin white hands of Aleardo's almost-brother
busying themselves with blessing the place as his perfectly
angelic voice, both suave and energetic, intoned a "Libera
nos Domine" rife with heartfelt determination and sense of
purpose.

This phrase from a ritual as old as the abyss itself was
accompanied by a few other sounds. There was a giggle from
the pretty Negro servant-girl who followed directly in the
wake of the altar boy with her hand clasped over her mouth,
fearful of losing further grip on her attempts to contain her
hilarity. A "shhh" came from Hipolito, whose severe and
attentive gaze allowed nothing to escape it. A gulp burgeoned
up from the sublimity of the bosom of the lady in pink. As far
as daughter was concerned, her face for the moment was
distinguished by a bare adumbration of disdain in the set of
her gracious lips, and an aura of annoyed incredulity. Her
eyes flashed their darkness at the emplumed and petrified
Master of the island, don Ilario Mendes-Segovia, regarding
him with a cordiality from which reproof hadn't completely
been expunged. The head of this American family, on the

other hand, seemed to be figuring just how much this theatrical production was costing him. It was not yet over, but he would have it pat to the very last cent all rung up on some invisible adding machine. The doubtful shake of his head during these "Libera" revealed a nature more managerial than spiritual.

After circling the perimeter of the room and finally pressing into its furthest, meanest corner where the creature's bedding lay in open confusion, the little group halted for moment, apparently disturbed. The noise of mothers's gulp, a little like the cry of a sea bird, grew thicker; the domestic's giggle and Hipolito's "shhh" whistled out again; and that serene, winged voice, after a pause which appeared to the Count to express a doubt, rose anew into the same invocation as before, the prelate's "Libera nos Domine," while the censer disgorged an authentic cloud of pardon and dispensation, yet somehow charged with an Oriental obscurity.

XI
The Fear of the Devil

New hypotheses.

Even though Aleardo's spirits were weighted with the heaviest oppression he had ever known, his anguish, luckily enough, was nearer to a boy's incomprehension in the face of disappointment and disillusion than to the bitterness of true despair, as was simply in keeping with his nature and his characteristic trust in life; this sense of oppression would in fact have resembled a great radiant smile in comparison to the feelings that would surely have been provoked in the Count if some magic had carried his gaze beyond the cellar, the hatchway, the kitchen, and the open door, and finally onto the path among the olive trees.

The much-tried Iguana, no less, was approaching from that direction, dawdling along absorbed in that half sad, half inattentive air typical of orphans, who typically cross the streets of life in attitudes of eternal questioning. After the Count had left her, she soon grew bored with her idiotic games, as though the stranger's interrogation and severe goodwill had served to reawaken her to the pain of her situation, fully reviving the worries the night had softened. She had forced the gate to the pen just a few minutes later and set out in barefoot silence to return to the house.

Despite being an Iguana—moreover of the gloomiest sort—Estrellita was afraid of moonlit nights with a fear that only her stronger fear of the Guzmans could temper, but still not destroy. Ever since her birth, or very nearly, they had always told her that monsters lurked everywhere, and you had better be careful. Later, when she had been broken to the round of domestic labors and her little green body, simply from exhaustion, became incapable of quaking before no matter what (which gave her at least the chance to sleep), the family's slow insinuations on the "physical" reality of the Lord of Evil (his actual incarnation in a particular individual they were careful not to name) had thrown the ice of authentic terror into her tiny mind. She lived with a horrible suspicion. After a period, initially, when it was simply unendurable, it now so deeply grieved her that she could not address it at all: the suspicion, almost the certainty, that she herself was the Devil—"the spirit of the shades," harried by the wrath of God.

This, along with yet another anguish you'll soon see brought to light, was the thorn that had stabbed itself into the *menina*'s mind and crazed her eyes with pain. While playing at night in the hen house, or trying to gain the sanctuary of her hole where the objects we have seen (including the plate of roasted seeds) somehow reassured her, she would be afraid of the silence of the moonlit night, but what truly held her in its grip was this unconfrontable terror of herself.

Now if instead of discussing this pitiful creature across distances to be measured in expanses of water and flights of days that now have turned into years, how would it be if we had been allowed that very night to walk the Iguana's path, suddenly to overtake her, and to hold her motionless for a moment by her thin green shoulders? We would have felt a first little tremor grow rigid into stony immobility, and those little eyes as they turned up to meet our own would have shone with no other light than the coldest desperation.

Anyone whom God has given a fate of continuous encounters with Evil has been dealt a terrible blow, though Catholics, of course, don't make the best example. For Catholics, Evil lies finally and exclusively in the absence of the Pleasures, whereas Protestants furnish a truer measure of the portent of really believing in the Devil, sometimes hanging him by the neck, sometimes cutting off his head, sometimes burning his body with billions of fiery sparks on a modernly invented chair. So, a terrible destiny has been allotted to people who have been thrown by God or their own ambitions (this is not yet clear) into continual conflict with perversity. But have you ever given a thought to the desperate plight of Perversity or Wickedness itself, deprived for virtually mathematical reasons of all possible struggle with itself, or of flight from itself, and therefore condemned to the constant horror of its own desperate presence, this presence being nothing other than itself? No, that's something you have never thought about.

And this isn't all. If you think you have focused on the maximum horror this fragile being could bear, you'll have to reconsider. The limit is yet to be reached, the achievement of the maximum still an open possibility. If one has been born within it, and nurtured, as it were, on its milk, there is no such thing as a horror that won't, in the course of time, transform itself, into habit and resigned indifference—surely a degraded kind of happiness, but a happiness all the same. But if someone is *later* recognized as the Devil himself and was not formerly considered such, having indeed been held to be something quite the contrary, worthy of kisses and caresses and gazed upon with happy blue-eyed smiles and every surrounding nuance singing a song of friendship and gentle consideration; if such a being were suddenly made to understand that there had been a monstrous error, that rather than loved as the incarnation of Good he was meant to be despised as the incarnation of Evil, shame, and wickedness, as the very Devil himself, and thus to be driven into a tunnel of solitude that can lead to no end but a gallows—you have to see that only such a creature, first revered as everything other than Evil and later decried as the Devil himself, only such a creature knows the whole mortal cold of Evil.

One thinks of hell as hot, a cauldron of pitch at zillions of degrees, but hell's true blazonry shows a minus- rather than a plus-sign; it's a place, Reader, of truly horrifying cold. And not only cold. It's a place of solitude: no one any longer speaks to you, and you yourself can speak to no one. Your mouth is shut up with a wall. This is Hell.

The little creature about whom our story revolves would sometimes forget this, and for the stupidest reasons imaginable: when she was alone and grasped a large red hen in her arms or found a brightly polished pebble, or if the olive trees sang or the March sun warmed the murmuring calm of the waters of the sea. But then a sense of desperation, where the despair of her current disgrace compounded with the memory that things had once been different, would collapse back down around her so secretly and subtly as to seem a forceps that had found its way into her tiny brain and set intently to ripping it out of her skull. Her pain grew buoyant and lifted her up, thrusting her outside of herself, and that was when she would get that cold little voice and that hard, unhealthy gaze, which were very strange to see in an animal, and then too she would lapse into that dark ardor of counting and burying the miserable coin with which her services were rewarded.

But now, Reader, we have had enough of reasoning about things that are all too dreary. The night, in Ocaña, has turned from red to blue; the sea is quiet; a light salt breeze rises from the beach, and our Iguana's wrinkled skin pulses with a shiver. Minuscule and solemn in her obscurity, the little creature who knew hope as but a mutilated stump has

94

set out towards home, or to what she had once called home. You'll imagine she was thinking who knows what kind of thoughts, but here again it is time to cast away illusions. She's only thinking she didn't make an accurate count of the stones of her last month's wages. There should have been thirty (while waiting for a raise), but she had been far too distracted in the afternoon when *o senhor* Hipolito counted them into her hand, and she has the impression she received no more than twenty-nine. She'll get her shovel, she imagines, dig up the treasure, and count it out again by the light of a candle.

Among so many expressions of inspirational sobriety, or malice, or even simple amusement, nothing yet uttered in the cellar had allowed the Count to grasp the central thread of it all, its explanation in terms of logic. The servant's den was receiving a benediction from a foreign Archbishop (leaving aside that the prelate was Aleardo's own almost-brother); one member of the Yankee family seemed to be suffering, another to be doing sums, another to be a goddess of flirtation (alluding here to the charming girl); the look on the Guzmans' faces made clear their responsibility for contriving the whole affair; but the Marquis at moments was at his summit of serenity and at others in the grip of his ferocious cycles of anguish and had all the air of having been dragged along rather than of pointing out the way. Once, when arrested by the girl's artful gaze, his eyes virtually pleaded: "Forgive me my dear for this stupid farce; it's only a rite and we have to bear with it for an older generation's peace of mind." It was on seeing this exchange, in fact, that the hidden guest finally felt a surge of enlightenment on the nature of this ceremony and began to unravel the subtle inter-relationships of the people taking part in it.

It was abundantly unmistakable that this young woman

must be the Marquis' *noiva*, just as the Count had already relinquished all doubt about the imminent closure of the sale of Ocaña, and of something or someone who stood for Ocaña. For the new proprietors to take charge of the house and the island itself could only highlight the Marquis—in concomitance moreover with the glory of his new-found feathers and the girl's enchanted glances—as the principle object of so many changes. And for the parents of the young man's favorite to be concerned about the property's former operation, and mostly about the ills it might conceal—the one of them preoccupied with the elimination of every residue of guilt and the other with pondering the total expense of such an enterprise—was nothing, as far as the Count could see, to be held up to blame. Undoubtedly, it all went back to that Perdita of the dedication, or to some other creature who had lived on the island previous to the Iguana's arrival—some creature with whom Perdita had hybridized in the Marquis' imagination. And in confessing his cult of the creature to the Archbishop (but how? and where?) Ilario had furnished him with sufficient pretext to demand a public disavowal. The Count remained perplexed only about how the Marquis' sense of dignity could allow such a desecration of his boyhood past, a kind of spiritual disinfection of the places where he had been closest to the angels, even despite a little oddness: the only access now allowed to such a precinct should be to smiling reminiscence and nostalgia. Primarily, then, the young man must be the victim of his future mother-in-law, a woman prepossessed with some notion of the sinfulness of youth, and of animality as necessarily distinguished by its lack of that highest good called the Soul. The Count on such a score would have expressed a number of doubts, considering that everything finds its source within one and the same great heart. It ought to follow that the destination of all hearts, no matter whether red, green, or azure, is most likely the same, which would also class them as all of equal goodness. It wasn't, of course, that he would go so far as to think of couplings between various species as in any way possible. That was clearly absurd. He simply saw a possibility for affectionate collaboration among the various species—affectionate collaboration and a common effort to rise above the terrestrial, which was surely what the Lord expected from all living creatures. From one shore to another of the wide grey ocean, someone must have sent a whisper of gossip and thoroughly reprehensible indiscretion about the Marquis' past fantasies, even perhaps alleging that a second little creature currently in the home of the aspiring groom had acceded to the privileges enjoyed by its predecessor! So we suddenly have a venerable prelate come scudding away from the Caribbean, hastening to Ocaña to reconsecrate the place. And that, clearly, was why the Iguana was banished from the house every evening.

The Count felt tired, finding this whole affair to resemble some tormented story out of Seventeenth Century Spain, and utter madness within the clarity of the present age; his body, moreover, was going stiff from his complicated posture in the closet, his perplexities about the island already had been resolved, and he had grown a little impatient with all of it. He decided to go to bed. The rest could wait until tomorrow when he would invite the good Archbishop to a frank and cordial discussion on the need to begin to abolish a few of the intimidatory manners still assumed by the Church. Immediately afterwards he would set sail for Milan. But just as he was about to withdraw, the trap door above the other hatchway lifted up, and he saw the appearance, one after the other, of two tiny shriveled green feet.

XII

Daddo Abandons the Closet

More coins. Daddo's dream.

The little servant was at the top of the stairs. She had passed through the kitchen, dreamlike, much as a person coming out of semi-obscurity will take in a sudden light as nothing more than a haze of bright confusion. Crouching, she felt her way down the steps. No matter what she might suspect, it was clear that she wouldn't for the moment have been able to see anyone.

This juncture, for the Count, was so grave that the young man pushed the covering of his hatchway completely aside— in no way bothering to be cautious—and prepared to make a rapid descent into the cellar so as to distract the attention of the assembled company from the poor miserable beast. But the onlookers were already so sharply affected by the appearance of the servant that it was of the figure of the Count, now outlined against the ceiling, that no one took notice, and the architect from Milan came to find himself seated on the topmost rung of his ladder in simple consideration of the unfolding of events. We can add that he removed his pipe from the pocket of his jacket, partly as a means of taking charge of his emotions and partly mechanically, but he didn't light it. This little operation too passed unremarked.

The Count could now relieve himself of any residual doubt he may have had about the truth of a time-honored observation on the absolute aplomb enjoyed by persons of exquisitely-bred manners, no matter how awkward the circumstances. On the faces of all the members of the group, and most particularly on the face of his almost-brother, since it was he who stood in the nearest distance, the Count saw the sudden formulation of expressions of calm and cordiality, some species of affected tenderness substituting for the agitated emotions that had gripped them no more than an instant before. Splendid civility stared out from the pupils of a good eighteen eyes, patiently following the renewed incarnation of Evil as she descended the stairs and directed her tiny steps towards the corner she was most familiar with, where her money was hidden in the ground. A scene of sheer perfection, marred only by the appearance of a great dark shadow that came to stand between the creature and the attainment of her goal: the shadow of the taciturn Hipolito, the brother of the rustic cook. He caught up with the creature and took her by surprise, grasping her like a cat by the scruff of the neck and hissing out a stream of softly modulated words:

"Since when has our Iguana learned to enter without knocking? Or perhaps you didn't see that ladies and gentlemen are in the room? So now you're downright unmannerly, added to the rest of the mischief you cause!" Then, turning to the guests, "I have to ask you to excuse us."

"Oh, but not at all!" exclaimed two or three voices at once, which were the voices, to be precise, of the Hopins family (since this, as we'll see in a moment, was who they were).

"I can see that Mrs. Hopins is very generous, and Mr. Hopins too," broke in Felipe. "Still, I want to assure our brother's soon-to-be mother- and father-in-law that our servants, in the past, weren't always so ill-mannered. The modern age has even reached Ocaña, and the help appears to have grown quite lax."

The Iguana now had understood everything; that was clear. With her little eyes wide open and brimming with an animosity so absolute that a veil seemed to have dropped in front of them, a mist of iron, she gave the impression of trying to get a bearing on the entirety of the room, while really seeing nothing. Hipolito's grip, moreover, had not let up.

"Leave her alone, don Hipolito," said don Fidenzio, judging that the moment had come for priestly intervention and inflecting a slight, suave melody in which the poor Lombard Count, with a shiver, could recognize the tones to which the members of the *haute* invariably make recourse when they find themselves in uncomfortable situations. The prelate spoke with an easy courtesy that contained not a trace of absolution. "Jesus, among the episodes of his divine predication, makes no mention of animals, and we can be certain that eternal life is none of their affair, since they have no souls. . . . But all the same, He never counsels us to hurt or maltreat them, since if the Heavenly Father created them, that must surely mean they serve some purpose. . . . Perhaps the unfortunate creature has come here in search of rest."

It was late, in fact, and the Iguana, for this as well as for no lack of other reasons, seemed unable to stand on her feet.

The Count had eyes—eyes, moreover, quite frankly bloodshot—almost exclusively for the daughter and mother of Evil, or for the personage who at any rate suspected that this is what she was; his attention was riveted to that most delectable of Iguanas, who was the joy of his heart. So he didn't really see the flicker of gay amusement over the lips of the queen of hearts or the desperation counterfeited into a smile on the face of the Marquis. He registered no more than the tail of it. But even to catch its tail, as it were, slumped him into still deeper melancholy.

The Negro domestic, in the meantime, on an order given

more by don Fidenzio's eyes than by his smile, which in truth showed signs of slippage, attempted to approach the Iguana, reaching out for her hand with a manner, as though from a tame to a savage animal, of crude affection; but the Iguana, suddenly awake again and irritated, declined quite brusquely with a vigorous shake of her snout.

"So now you even bite," came the words of Felipe, making fun of her.

In a whisper, Mr. and Mrs. Hopins took the moment as propitious for exchanging a few observations which, judging from their smiling glances and overly-honeyed tones, might have concerned any subject at all except the Iguana. Looking up to address the Archbishop, they in fact informed him of their impression, "at first glance," that these basements were just the sort of space required for a good, modern heating system and ought to be sufficiently ample "for all the piping and the furnace." Of course, they would need the confirmation of a decent architect.

This reticence, like the rest of this sudden disclaiming of the meaning of the scene, including the motivations that had brought these people together to form it, bore a touch of something so false and clumsy that even don Fidenzio found it embarrassing. He went along with the game while intending all the same to be clear, yet not overly clear, which was also a way of pursuing goals of his own. He admitted:

"Anything and everything is possible, as long as it reflects God's will and if our hearts sincerely request it. It seems to me that the villa, by now, is perfectly inhabitable, in the sense I'm sure you will intuit, but only on condition, naturally enough, that no excessive sensibility on the part of the new inhabitants shall come to constitute a compromise of such a highly desirable conclusion."

"Now, I think I'd like to hear that plainer, please, Mon

-signor," chimed in Mr. Hopins, with a purely Yankee turn of phrase. "You don't really understand my wife, and now you've got her worried."

"I am saying that the house, by the grace of God, is now *inhabitable:* repainted from top to bottom, thoroughly remodernized, and with a corner dedicated here and there to the Virgin and always gladdened by the flowers that the hands of the new Marquesa will be happy to pick, it will doubtless seem even gay and joyful; but the shadows will disappear *only with time and prayer.*"

"I can assure you, *o senhor,*" Hipolito broke in almost rudely, addressing himself to Mr. Hopins with a kind of bored irritation, "that the Archbishop's words are full of judiciousness, and his sense of scruple does him credit; but still, well, the creature doesn't merit so much attention. She never did anything really evil; and she may have a dismal air, but that's natural to these primordial sorts of beasts, and it doesn't exclude her being innocuous."

Don Fidenzio swallowed back an expression of dismissal, from which the Count understood that the *legend* of the house, for some very inscrutable reason, was very seriously on his mind; but this feeling struck him only superficially since he also appeared to have gathered— and with a passionate stab of pain despite being still unable to believe his impression—that the present scene revolved not around the distant Perdita but rather, for some motive he hoped would prove to be of little substance, around his Iguana! And he could not see how that was possible.

"Fine . . . fine, then," responded Mr. Hopins, while throwing a cold, furtive glance at the animal who stood there, head bowed, with a vaguely equivocal light in her tormented smile. "If that's the way you see it. . . . I couldn't ask for more. . . . So let's go now, Helene. . . . But what's wrong with you?"

A perfectly opportune question, since the very limit of the stress and terror incumbent upon the future mother-in-law of a poet of don Ilario's sickly sort—upon a loving mother whom only the divine authority of the Church could persuade to accept the horror of such a contamination of the fruit of her womb—that limit for Mrs. Helene Hopins had been reached, the cup drunk to the dregs. Almost as though her mind could literally accept no more (there had also been the strain of trying to cope with the never-before-imagined but now actual appearance of the beast), she was clearly emitting the signs of an hysterical collapse both imminent and spectacular: a sudden, ulterior lengthening of her already long person; a backwards leaping of her flowered hat; eyes that dropped completely shut, but not in time to prevent an abundant shedding of tears; her mouth, previously clamped tight around a meaningful-sounding "hmmmm," suddenly burst open with:

"Enough of this! Enough of it! Take that thing away and kill it."

She tumbled then into the encircling arms of Mr. Hopins and of their very pretty daughter.

Two long strong hands, the hands now of Felipe the cook, snapped out to take hold of the personification of Evil, or the servant, or the little Iguana once again, this time by the shoulder; but there was only an instant's uncertainty (while those in her nearest vicinity heard a sharp grinding of two small teeth) before she tore free of the gentleman and fled. And where, Reader, would she flee if not, like the terrified mouse, to the place of least protection, which is to say to the feet of the Marquis of Segovia? And what would he do if not step aside—no more than an inch, but still step aside—and turn a stony smile towards his queen of hearts? So Felipe's grip reached the beast-girl still again, and she fled again and ran to hide, *growling*—that's precisely the word, or sobbing perhaps as well, but the growl was much plainer—in her little corner, the lair where she kept her pebbles or pieces of money, and where Felipe, again right behind her, flailed out a kick in her direction but missed and sent all the little stones flying, or a least a good part of them; at dusk, when he had called her, she had forgotten to bury them. They scattered here and there while a laugh, at first uncertain but then quite general, brought the remarkable scene to a close.

As Mrs. Hopins reascended the steps to the kitchen with the help of her lord and personal domestic—Mr. Hopins served the function of both—and with the immediate rear brought up by a Marquis so anxious that he seemed to be looking for escape, and lastly by don Fidenzio, a little circle formed around the Iguana, who drew herself up to her knees and began to collect her treasures. At first she seemed suspicious or fearful of the people standing around her, but that slipped away and she was simply crazed or utterly indifferent. The youthful eyes of the future Marquesa and the black domestic reflected little if any amusement, and they looked on with ill-concealed compassion, more than anything else, while embarrassment and contempt marked the scowling faces of the Avaredo brothers. No more sounds of laughter. Only the short, dry pants from the throat of the Iguana.

"Alright, Estrellita, it's time to calm down!" called Hipolito, in a low voice that nonetheless showed signs of strain—a voice in which the Count identified a shade of pity that allowed him some residual hope for the salvation of Hipolito's soul. "Calm down, and go to bed. You know you have to be ready. *O senhor* Cole will be coming to get you in the afternoon."

Miss Hopins observed, "But . . . she thinks that's money? How strange. . . ."

"Because she's a strange creature, *o senhora*, even if she's not really bad. She's very greedy; she'd never stop hoarding things up. She has a mania about money."

Why the Count didn't rise from his perch at the top of the ladder, go down among these people and take his protégée by the hand, makes for a riddle that only his affection for the little Iguana can explain. He was completely bewitched by her sufferings and solitude, by her horrifying intensity and her fantasies, by the unreal, painfilled reality she lived in, and as well by all the family's shameful ridiculous mystifications, from the cowardice (which is what it had to be called) of Mendez the Marquis to the authoritarian violence of his brothers, and now there was even the discovery that Estrellita's childhood on Ocaña was finished forever, that they'd be coming to take her away tomorrow, throwing her into a strange and unknown world, perhaps into the house of some parvenus along the coast. He had been so unseated from his normally Olympian calm by all these particulars of the monument to evil (evil as the manipulation of stupidity and innocence) which the island of Ocaña was erecting beneath his unseen eyes, as to be overcome now by a form of pain—and here, Reader, you are not to be surprised, since he was only a human being—not dissimilar to drowsiness. He didn't wake back up to himself until the cellar was once again in darkness, except for a green reflection of moonlight falling through the hatchway. The silence, moreover, was so limpid that he wasn't afraid, as he descended, of disturbing anyone.

With the help of that greenish light he made his way into the corner where the Iguana had scrunched herself up, and he saw that the creature, doubled against the wall with a paw pressed to her head, was perfectly immobile. His fear she was weeping disappeared when he realized that the "grr-grr" issuing from her throat wasn't a wail, but the nasal breathing of children whose crying has cried itself out and allowed them to fall asleep. One little eye was closed, the other half-open

105

staring fixedly—the Count might have said "reprovingly." But he suffered from a simple optical illusion, because his mind no longer had a firm grasp on things.

Aleardo stood in contemplation of the Iguana for quite some time, and the expression on his face, so strong and absorbed, was something his dearest boyhood friends had never seen, nor even the girls of May. Then, after fantasizing freely on the cozy room full of carpets, delicacies, and toys that he would prepare for her in his mansion in Milan (he no longer though of entrusting her to nuns), and on the serenity and joy that would now fill up the entirety of the life of the beast, tomorrow and forever, he again traced his way to the ladder, the trap door, the guest room. He lay down on the bed, completely dressed, and after a while, for now he was truly tired, he dropped into deep sound sleep.

The Storm

XIII

On the Beach

The voices behind the wall. Deceived! The good Cavalier.

He woke up feeling cold, but also calm, as we typically remember an acrid pain after the passage of many years; he had rested so completely in the solitude of those few short hours before dawn that his mind saw the events of the previous day and night as having receded into an enormous distance, so far away (or so he believed) as to appear to have shed all weight. Out of the window, which he had left wide open (the cause of his chill), he could also see that it had rained during the night, just as he had imagined it would; and now it continued to drizzle, but so lightly that at moments it seemed no more than humidity. The sky was grey yet quite high, which kept it from being somber, and there was a silvery brightness in the air, a touch of white or grey, absolutely still: in a word, it was the very same air one breathes in Milan when winter is about to end, somewhere between fresh and damp, as though traversed in its peacefulness by a thought. This lent the Count, in harmony with the banality of the voices that filtered through the wall from the adjacent room, an almost boring feeling of tranquillity, as though his trip had been marked by nothing special, and he found himself on the verge of thinking only about the hour at which to return to the *Luisa* and hoist anchor; he could see the sail begin to swell, and the reappearance of the much-loved turrets of the Duomo in Milan. He smiled quite contentedly. But little by little those voices, all the same, began to grow clearer and to capture his interest.

"Can't you see she didn't do it on purpose, poor creature, barging in like that while all of us were there?" sounded the Marquis' voice. "I'm certain too that Mrs. Hopins didn't take it badly. She had a terrible headache because of the service and merely wanted to get back to the boat as quickly as possible."

"Keep on fooling yourself, dear brother, about the ingenuousness of your mother-in-law. She's as sharp as the Devil himself, and a woman of character. I can tell you you're badly mistaken if you imagine she'll ever set foot in here again," Felipe's voice objected, full of sarcasm, "and you can thank that little whore for that."

"I really cannot go along with your choice of words," the Marquis responded, his voice trembling with tears. "She . . . she never did anything awful, and I have told you that a thousand times; it's just that she was fond of me. If only she had remained with my mother, who was a woman of strength! Weaklings corrupt everything, because they use everything, and that's all it makes sense to say; then they grow up to hate the creatures or things they've used, despising and rejecting them without thinking about the fates they have to face."

Then silence, but a silence that the Count, petrified, found charged with possibility. It gave issue, however, to only a few muffled words:

HIPOLITO: "*O senhor* Cole has promised to get here around two in the afternoon, if the weather doesn't turn bad. . . ."

DON JERONIMO (since this was picture of Ilario that now rose to the Count's mind), speaking with equal lack of intensity: "Tell her she's going on an outing. . . . That she'll soon be coming back to Ocaña. . . . If she asks for me, tell her I'm busy. I don't want to see her."

HIPOLITO: "Don Fidenzio is a man of the world. According to me, he has already managed to convince the family of your innocence."

DON JERONIMO-ILARIO: "For all that matters to me . . ."

FELIPE: "It'll matter to you, brother, it'll matter."

Just these few words, followed by nothing more.

After a considerable, inexplicably long wait, the Count got up and busied himself, fairly superficially, with washing and dressing. There were times when his soul experienced moments of emptiness and what we would call absolute distance. This, now, was one of those moments.

Entering the dining room shortly afterwards, he observed that no one was there; only a cup of coffee and a roll, abandoned on the table, attested to the Guzmans' having distractedly remembered their guest from Milan. But he left them untouched and went out, pensively, into the open air.

He walked along the beach, paying no heed to the light rain, and felt unspeakably relieved to encounter no sign of life except the *Luisa* which, moreover, showed no lights and no activity. He was now, Reader, in the grips of a particularly unpleasant feeling, and it was whatever you choose to call that feeling with which frank and trusting hearts are afflicted when confronted with proof, or seeming proof, of having been deceived. More than wounded by the Marquis' tortured psychology, the Count was pained by his confrontation with the duplicity (judging from what he had heard) in the character of the enchanting Iguana. So she wasn't so simple a little beast as he had previously believed. She could even, so it seemed, be compared to the figure of what amounted to a true human being, no matter how depraved. She had taken Perdita's place! The phrases around the gentlewoman who had reared both of these lower creatures had spoken quite clearly. "How did I manage not to realize it? Why didn't I see?" Daddo said to himself. "Am I really such a fool? So completely backwards?" Yes, he truly upbraided himself with such reproofs, even while a voice from a more reasonable corner of his heart counselled him not to be so upset, since such blindness is comprehensible. One has to remember, too, that only the greatest philosophers and most elevated scholars can begin (perhaps) to tell us where the animal ends and where the true human being commences; to say nothing, then, of the way such differentiations grow ever more tenuous with the flowering of civilization, and of how one is often uncertain as to which of the two castes is encroaching upon the other. Finally, continuing along his line of reasoning, the Count grew calm again, having reached the juncture, perhaps somewhat arbitrary, that the human consists of everything that can voice a lament, whereas subhumanity (or animal life) comprises everything that refuses to assuage that lament, not to mention the things that provoke it. So the only course under certain given circumstances, if one isn't to incur the risk of running counter to something human, is to rush toward the places from which lamentation can be heard to issue, and then to extirpate its cause but still with no meting out of punishment, indeed attempting to give succour to those who had been its determinant. Since they no longer lay within the order of things, but outside and even against it, they too had to be numbered among the victims of suffering. If the little Iguana wasn't entirely or any longer a simple little Iguana—which was something, if we are not to be afraid of the truth, that Aleardo had already half-way suspected—and if this could be attributed to some natural course of evolution, why shouldn't one find a joy in that? And if the Marquis for his part (due again to some natural phenomenon) were in the opposite situation—if he were ceasing, that's to say, to be a human being, let alone a Marquis (didn't all his tremblings amount to just this much?)—why shouldn't one give him help? Clearly he wasn't a criminal or a person of wickedness.

The Count now caught sight of Ilario—could it be that the boy had arrived to offer him the confirmations he so in tensely desired?—and what he saw was enough to persuade him, at least for the space of an instant, of the justice of this new conviction just grown clear in his mind. Approaching from the other side of the beach and carrying a book in his hand, Ilario showed a face so mild and joyful, with something pure and inspired in his eyes, that all the feelings of friendship that had flowered in the heart of the Count during his first encounters with this poor unfortunate suddenly reappeared, like the revival of a smile.

At this point, Reader, we can no longer hide what you yourself, as a person of sensibility, will already have intuited: our Aleardo, with his noble mien, open forehead, friendly manners, and most of all with his extraordinary proclivity for reasoning things out, was himself a person of little self-assurance. He was in need of a mother, a lover, or a brother whom life had not given him, even though he had been regaled with the appearance of a fine and limpid destiny. What finally made him so devoutly concerned with everything around him, and simultaneously so distant, even in the midst of literary company in Milan, was precisely his certainty of being a cipher, a nothing, an uninhabited consciousness, a water-filled cloud that would soon dissolve. His finely-bred sense of *savoir-faire*, this alone, previously had saved him from finding his condition a source of constant suffering; but now the subtle terror of life had reared itself up to stare him in the face and made him more desirous than ever for a kind word, a smile, or one of those handshakes that fill

113

one with hope. So he looked at the ineffable Marquis as no friend ever before had looked at a friend, as no child had ever regarded its mother.

His hopes did not last long. As the younger man advanced, the Count inquired further than the expressions we have already pointed out and he saw something different and deeper, an expression hinging by turns on falsity, death, an irremediable disgust with the self. His very smile (the Count's) —we won't say it actually expired, but no peace or hope continued to stir inside of him. He was left with only his aptitude for polite and dreamy distance.

"So this is where you are, Daddo," spoke the Marquis, after offering his hand, but very superficially. He appeared not really to seen the Count. He didn't even add "Did you sleep well?" or some other conventionally courteous phrase, and he remained entirely unaware of the Lombard's mute melancholy. Opening his volume to a page that looked considerably worn and tortured by his fragile fingernails, he continued as though neither the beach, nor the rainy morning, nor any other aspect of reality existed around the two of them.

"Listen to this. I'd like you to hear these verses by Captain Jorge Manrique on the death of his father, the Master of Santiago; and then tell me if it isn't God Himself who puts such words across our path when we find ourselves at a crossroads and with our hearts full of questions. I found this book under the kitchen sink, quite by chance. I thought I had lost it. . . ." The sadness of the gaze he turned to the Count contained his certain knowledge—yet still it seemed to him an impossible thing—that Aleardo was fully abreast of his problems and capable of understanding him. He looked at the Count with unaccountable weirdness, as if begging concession of grace and salvation, and then began to read:

In his city of Ocaña,
Death came to knock
at the door,

    saying, "Good Cavalier,
take leave of this faulted world
and its goods;
let the steel of your heart
show its untamed strength
in the crossing;
    and since you have held
both life and health of slight account
in favor of fame,
let virtue nerve your heart
to suffer the affront
that calls you.

    "Think not of the frightful battle
you await
as overly bitter,
since a life all the longer
for glorious fame
is what you leave behind you.
    Even the life of honor
is neither eternal nor true
though, all the same, far better
than that other, temporal
and quick to perish. . . ."

As don Ilario recited these verses, his face, while still
the mixture of falsity, suffering, and humiliation, seemed
once again, as the previous night on the balcony, slowly to
disappear and dissolve within a succession of identical faces,
each one younger, purer, and more luminous than the one

before, and so free of all signs of decay, and as well of the murky enchantment of the moonlit night, as to be comparable to the face of an angel. His friend, the Count, while asking himself why he found these verses so sweet and yet upsetting, achieved a clear, unperturbed perception of just how great the Marquis' spiritual beauty must have been before the dullness of aging, a consequence of fear, had taken hold of him, and before a mere human weakness had gone into hiding behind the desire to avoid payment of the price it had to cost. Therefore:

"What did you say?" asked the Count, through a blinking of reddened eyes. "Excuse me, but I haven't understood very well. The cavalier received some invitation, but to what?"

"I'll read it to you again," responded the Marquis without hesitation; but he could no longer find the page since he had removed his index finger from the book while reciting, and some curious tension now rose over his face—virtually as though his memory were failing him—while the morning wind moved a few long whitish strands of hair across his forehead. As he once again turned old, he quietly stated:

"You could say that this cavalier was a fundamentally good man, but had come to find himself at a crossroads, since it was time for him to die, but he was still attached to life; and Death encourages him to put an end to the question by making a choice. He's told he should lovingly choose Death and willingly follow it, and that he shouldn't try to choose life, since life no longer has any need of him."

As the young man spoke these words, his eyes filled with tears.

XIV
Daddo Listens

A brief invitation to freedom. The definition
of the diabolical.

While sometimes he listened to these words, and sometimes didn't—distracted by his pity for those strands of blond
hair and that death-mask of a face, and again by the nebu-
lous delicacy of the sky, and even further by the figure he
vaguely, almost unconsciously watched as it rowed a dinghy
towards the beach, this being don Fidenzio—Daddo was also
rediscovering his fealty to that primitive, almost leaden tenderness of the true Lombard, such as we were able to trace it
out at the beginning of this story: a severe and almost stupid
simplicity of heart that asks God no questions, awaiting only
His orders and then giving them execution with infantile
sense of scruple. He once again felt a stirring of that passionate sense of devotion, both filial and paternal, with which he
habitually addressed himself to everything; he almost found
that all creatures everywhere were eternally dependent upon
his strengths, that he personally had been entrusted to bend
his body over them in unflagging acts of protection and
vigilance. Thus, having taken that book of ancient poems
with his left hand, he discovered himself gripping the Marquis' thin arm with his right, and appealing to him in a voice
both soft and nonetheless firm within a register of calm benevolence.

117

"Perhaps I am being indiscreet; and if I am, I hope you'll excuse my clumsiness, since it comes from having to deal with a frankly pressing question. How, my dear, can I be of use to you? I'm not ashamed to offer a list of the things I possess, since they don't actually belong to me and have been lent from above: will-power, health, the little learning I've acquired, the properties my father left me, and the esteem I enjoy in the country I come from. I want to put it all at your disposal, if only you'll make an exchange. What I want you to give me in return is whatever it is that causes you such despair. Perhaps I'm deceiving myself, but I believe you were born a free individual, and you can be free once again."

The Marquis' reply, no matter how softly, came from a man beside himself with rage:

"Free! What's that supposed to mean? Can freedom come from anywhere outside of us? Can it be anything other than the fruit of a violence we have to inflict upon all our desires for a life that's secure and comfortable? Can it make any peace with an ideal of a life relieved of the weight of responsibility, when it's a question too of responsibilities that we ourselves have freely assumed?"

"But perhaps not freely; that's my point," rejoined the Count, thoughtfully studying the younger man's forehead. "Sometimes we take on responsibilities, like debts, without really knowing the total they'll amount to. And at that point there would surely be no justice in allowing a debtor to be ruined merely because solvency is beyond his possibilities. That's all I meant to say, my friend."

"Oh, my shoulders would willingly carry all the debts of the world and of every other world as well, all of them except for one!" The Marquis almost screamed.

Simply, but again in the dry Lombard manner, the Count posed the question:

"Which one, Ilario? Please, which one?"

"That's something I cannot possibly tell you," replied the poet, his face convulsing into a smile.

"But why?" was the Count's pained reply, seeing that vandalized smile as proof of the damages which a freedom unchecked by any knowledge of the rights of others had wreaked on Ilario's soul, driving it to an otherwise incomprehensible desperation. He also wondered, with a wince, if the friendship he himself professed were perhaps no more than empty chatter.

"Because . . . well, because that's the way things stand." The expression was less childish, but the Marquis' reply had been practically the same as the Iguana's.

They walked on for a few minutes without speaking.

The Count was in a fury as he had seldom been before, with an anger no less silent than rapid; at one moment he imagined informing the Marquis of everything he knew about him; in the next to return again to supplications; in the next again to proffer a cold good-by and immediately set back out to sea; within his soul a medley of voices rose up like doves from a threatened nest and begged him to retrace his steps. But Aleardo paid them no attention. This then was the complex state of mind in which he found himself when the new rowboat snapped suddenly into focus, running up onto the beach and allowing the landing, amid that pearly glitter of the sea, of the red-and-black but virtually unsmiling protégé of his grandmother the dowager countess.

The younger man had also seen him and his face had gone whiter than air. The flush of vexation on don Fidenzio's visage, and something that seemed to make the prelate's eyes an announcement of new and unsettling developments, gave Ilario immediately to understand that the so-much feared and yet hoped-for breaking of the engagement had already taken place. His heart made no stint of its approval, yet he had the feeling that the blood was in flight from all of his veins. He was tormented too by another worry, as sharp as a flaming sword: how could he justify the arrival of the prelate in the eyes of his friend, which was a question really of having to explain a relationship that from the very first greeting would reveal itself to be anything other than fortuitous. Even as Aleardo watched him, aware of the problem and thoroughly discomfitted by his host's predicament, Ilario made the decision weak men always make: he would ignore the danger until it bore down directly upon him. Fortunately, however, Aleardo's very presence was enough to divert such a danger, at least momentarily, from his poor disconsolate head. As the prelate raised his eyes and directed them to the two young men standing before him, he unhesitatingly recognized the taller, more modernly dressed of them to be none other than the not really predilected grandson of the woman who had shown him the attentions of a mother; and since his soul, over a good number of years by now, was often perturbed by interior voices which upbraided him for his various traffickings, the scene he faced seemed less a reality than a purificatory vision that had come to impart the warnings of the great lady of Como. He stopped in his tracks and remained for a longish moment in what might have been taken for a sudden ecstasy, giving the master of the island just the time he needed to reclaim his wits. In a mixture of terror and remorse, but seasoned with a certain archaic coldness, Ilario guided the Count to a small damp hollow behind a rise that ran back obliquely from the shore and across the beach—a hollow where a tongue of grey water in a tidal pool washed over a bed of smooth pebbles, pale blue and green. Daddo looked at him with commiseration.

"When you have left this place," the Marquis resumed, now kneeling down both to hide his violent emotions and the shaking of his hands and to pick up a small blue stone he then intently studied, "When you've left this place, Daddo, try not to think badly of me. This is something I have already told you: a great deal of squalor is hidden among these islands, but not all of it is voluntary or ignoble." He looked at the bluish pebble as though about to cry, and the Count unavoidably associated the small flat stone with all of those others collected by the island's ill-fated servant, the Iguana; and he understood, even without really understanding, why such stones were so dear to the sweet little beast. "Will you be leaving early?" continued Ilario, now again seeming to be Jeronimo. Conceivably he was trying to rouse his courage, or at least to give an imprint of courage to his voice.

Aleardo was no longer listening. Then he became aware of having been asked a question and replied, seeming to speak across a distance:

"I imagine . . . rather late in the afternoon."

"Then take this stone. I have nothing else to give you by which to remember me."

Aleardo took the stone; but as he opened his wallet to put it away, the corner of his eye spied the reappearance of don Fidenzio, gesturing in surprise against the grey backdrop of the sea. This vision, perhaps inexplicably, took Daddo back to his childhood, and from there to Milan, and then to all his high-flown precepts on the necessity of action. With a sudden sense of shame, he focused on just how much time he had lost in preliminary elucubrations about how best to up-root an anguish, almost weighing the possibility of allowing it franchise. His manner now gone cold and dry, he tossed the pebble sharply back into the sea, saying:

"You aren't yet dead, and I have no need to mourn for you, since what I truly feel for you is love. And now, my friend, you have to listen to me: I'm going to make you a proposal."

Don Ilario-Jeronimo just barely wrinkled his forehead

while watching the trajectory of the stone as it fell into the water; and his pique, as it appeared to the Count, was surely at odds with his previous affirmations. He might have given the impression that bemoaning his state was really much dearer to him than the liberation he dreamed of. This detail did not escape the Count, who preferred however to ascribe it to the affection that unfortunates, as time goes by, conceive for their own undoing. It excited his solidarity all the more.

"We've already spoken," continued the Count, "about the publishing situation in Milan, and I don't want to hazard an opinion on its real significance, or the lack of it: I only know it represents a course of action, and, as such, an incitement to life and the assumption of the kinds of responsibilities that alone turn a boy into a man. So I want you to come to Milan, my friend, and you're to set out today, with me. You'll discover it to offer not a few, but in fact a great many ways of making use of your talents as a man of culture and sensitivity. And if your soul contains sadness and regrets, living with other people will teach that all of us have these sorts of things in common. Action itself is extremely purifying, and combined with the possibility of doing good for others it will give you the patience, little by little, that a man has to have to live down his sins, if a sin, moreover, is something you have ever committed."

Just as on the previous day, when they were seated at table, the Marquis contracted with a shudder, the way a man reacts to the bite of a flea on his shoulder. He muttered:

"I already said this yesterday, and don't like repeating it, but it's late for me now, very late, I'm afraid."

He looked up, beside himself with commotion, towards the figure of the Monsignor.

The Count too was observing the Monsignor, but without in any way seeming to, and above all—since Daddo knew everything about the man from his childhood onward including his most recent occupations—without interest. Thus, with just the slightest hitch in his voice, but with as well the obstinate supplication of the true believer, he continued:

"I have money aboard the boat, really somewhat more than serves my needs, and I'll be grateful if you'll help me get rid of it. Sooner or later I'll be able to manage by myself, but for now, if you can see your way to complying, I'd like you please to accept a good part of it as an advance. . . . It will be of help to you."

"An advance . . . against what?" asked the planet-struck Marquis, unable to withdraw his gaze, now gone glassy, from don Fidenzio, who was stepping along the stones, just barely lifting the skirts of his gown to keep it out of the water, and approaching ever closer.

"Against the royalties from your poems. . . . You already know that," answered the Count.

"Ah, if only I could believe I had written, not a poem, but a single line that had some value for the history of Portugal, I'd die a happy death right now," was the young man's reply. "But here I am, after so many years of such a glorious illusion, and it's not my books to be found on the market, but me. . . . I myself am up for sale!" What had issued from his throat was virtually a wail.

The Count, feeling unspeakably ashamed with the very same shame he always felt when he came upon creatures tied down or incapable of wriggling free of their bonds—a shame not for them, but for himself, since he was free—found it difficult to speak; then, with a calm the source of which was a mystery even for him:

123

"I see that the sea isn't good this morning, and shows a kind of restlessness. So I'll now go aboard to get the wherewithal I've just been speaking about. In the meanwhile, my friend, I hope, please, that you'll give some thought to my proposal, and if you see your way to accepting it we'll leave at two this afternoon. In any case, prepare me a clean, correct copy of your works and a proxy giving me authorization to act on your behalf. Go, now, my boy, let's waste no more time."

"And can you promise me," replied the Marquis in a state of great agitation, "not to listen to any rumors or appearances that may seem to work against me and the unfortunate life I've led? I sometimes have the impression that even the shadows take on substance, and even the wind wears the hat of a priest. But it's not me, no, it's not me who's to be denounced as the Devil!"

"Neither you nor anyone else; the only thing to deserve that name is uncontained purchasing power," replied the Count to himself, then adding aloud, "Yes, I can make that promise." As the younger man turned and left the place at a run, with the bearing of something lacerated and frightened— it was a sight to arouse one's pity—the Count found himself dreamily repeating those lines by Captain Jorge Manrique:

> Think not of the frightful battle
> . . . .
> as overly bitter
> since a life all the longer
> for glorious fame. . . .

Meantime, don Fidenzio was approaching, ever more surprised, and finally called out:

"Is that you, dear Aleardo? Can it be you, my charming boy? I thought you were an hallucination. . . . How is your mother, the Countess?"

But:

In his city of Ocaña
. . . .
. . . ."Good Cavalier,
take leave of this faulted world
and its goods. . . ."

was all the Count could hear distinctly, mixed with the more
lively sound of the sea, in which the voice of the prelate, with
all its gaiety, sounded somehow desperate. These were the
noblest words the Count had ever heard. He was like a man
who had traversed the entirety of a life always trying to remember some angelic tune that would carry him back to the
first time he fell in love, or else to who knows what. Now he
had it inside of him. His emotions were so strong that he
couldn't add a smile to the intense and serious expression on
his face; walking past the prelate, fixing him as though the
only thing in his place were a scattering of spray and wind,
he directed himself to his own rowboat, lowered the oars, and
set off towards the open sea.

XV
The Little Star

Happiness. The fall. Abject dissimulations.

Turning aside for a moment from these two Lombard gentlemen (the one of them intent upon guiding his rowboat across the endless pallor of the sea towards the not-distant *Luisa,* and the other suddenly bewildered as he asked himself whether the figure he had seen was man or ghost and why don Ilario had fled, all of it making him suspicious now of the one of them, now of the other, and finally again of the firmness of his very own mind, even to the point of imputing a guilt, little as he liked to do so, to his own cupidity), we find our way back to the primal cause of so much dilemma, our Estrellita of the Caribes, the island's woe-begone servant, in precisely the moment when she began to return to consciousness— rather a dim affair—of herself and the world, and to stir again in the darkness of the corner with which you are already acquainted.

Even before she opened her little eyes and realized she had fallen asleep with her head propped against the wall, the complicated circle of her terrors had again resumed its motions within this tiny daughter of evil.

It consisted really of a series of circles to which you might just as easily refer as days, months, and even years, compounded out of absolute emptiness. But the remotest of these circles, now faded and dull, was a simple ray of October sunshine in which the Marquis' angelic head—he was little more than a boy at the time—had the gravity and benignity of a god, let alone of a man. In this now distant place, certain lights that found their source in the inexhaustible blue of his eyes told the Iguana she was very dear to him: that she was a part of his soul, by now belonged to the human family, and no longer had to crawl along the earth and die. The little Iguana, elevated out of her animal condition by what the Marquis saw in her, or thought he saw, was no longer a lizard with a sad, thin green body, but a genteel and delightful daughter of man. The Marquis strolled along the beach with her, offering her his arm, precisely as though she were a miniscule lady, and he leaned his head towards her narrow muzzle, repeatedly calling her "my little star." The Iguana was beside herself with pride and satisfaction. Never from the time of her birth had she looked at herself in a mirror, but that didn't matter: she knew she was beautiful, and now extremely beautiful, and as for every daughter of mankind her beauty was a beatification. Everything she did, her every step, each and every one of her unassuming, uncontrived, and unconscious actions, seemed to give the Marquis more pleasure than spring itself or a regal crown.

The brothers, in this period, simply don't exist. The only thing that exists is the Marquis, her Daddy, or something even more than that: something our little Iguana, in her absolute stupidity, is unable to catalog, but the name of it is gentleness and the hope of being forever transformed into a charming little star. Because the Marquis had promised that one day when she was grown he'd take her to paradise, a very large place beyond the sea, where he'd present her as his bride and everyone would honor her and she would know "*a happiness you can't even imagine.*"

"But I don't need anything more than what I have,

Daddy; I swear it," laughed the little Iguana in reply and with a great strange joy in pronouncing this word the Marquis seemed so much to like to hear.

"You'll see I'm making no mistake. Let your Daddy take care of things; he knows what he's up to. . . ."

"Yes . . . yes, Daddy."

The Iguana's heart, at the time, was as warm and dark as a seed hidden in the ground beneath good earth. She knows a fine blue flower is about to bloom, before not too long now, fine and blue and eternal as well, so she has no need to be in a rush; but her every step, glance and tone of voice, even when she sleeps, is a song of praise, a passionate expression of gratitude to the Daddy among daddies, the Marquis among marquis:

"I've been born through you. . . ."

"You are all I live for. . . ."

"So kind and wise. . . ."

"You'll be taking me to paradise, tomorrow. . . ."

"Where I'll see you in all your glory. . . ."

"Me, your little servant. . . ."

(Here we have taken a cursory glance, no more, at how the Segovia-Iguana relationship had stood until only a few years before: and we're to see that both the idyll and its collapse took place *before* the Portuguese nobleman fell ill.)

In the desert where his little servant later came to find herself and where she could no longer call out to him nor make herself heard in any other way, the silence is completed only by the voice of the day when the Marquis summoned her, while his brothers slept, to the place where he was seated beneath the great oak tree and then announced:

"Now, little Iguana, things are different between you and me. I want you to stay out of my sight as much as possible. You've already done me quite enough harm."

"Me?" said the little Iguana. She laughed, thinking he was playing some joke.

"Who else?" said the Marquis. "Do you think perhaps I'm talking to myself?"

"But what kind of harm?" replied the Iguana without in any way understanding.

"I've aged. I'm about to die."

"Daddy," cried the Iguana, who sometimes addressed the Marquis with this word in moments when it was even less intelligent than usual to do so, "Daddy, but you haven't gotten old, and you can't die."

"And that's where you're wrong, and it's all your fault. Your beastliness and essential nothingness have cut me off from everything happy and wonderful that ought to be due to me out of birth, beauty, genius, and distinction. You've brought me to perdition, a nothing that owns nothing to offer. Now get away from me, you filth of a little woman!"

"I . . . what do you mean, Daddy?"

"So you want to pretend you don't understand. . . . Which makes you a liar too."

"But Daddy, I never tell lies, I don't know what you want to say," replied the little Iguana, falling onto her knees before the young gentleman and speaking in a barely audible voice.

"And don't call me Daddy, because I have never been anybody's Daddy, and thank God there's still time for that! So get away from me now! You're a total stranger and I can't stand the sight of you."

"Yes, Daddy."

Hell for the little Iguana (and likewise, we'll quickly add, for the Marquis, who had spoken these words with horrendous suffering and a feeling of great pity for the Iguana, but who had also been left no choice after the receipt of a certain letter from Merida) had begun on precisely that day; and it wasn't, unfortunately, an experience for which the beast was prepared. She fell sick for some time, and when they came to rouse her it was to entrust her with the bucket for the well and to tell her (these are Ilario's brothers) that the Marquis was ill and didn't want to be spoken to by any *outsiders*; the family, moreover, had fallen on harder times during these illnesses and now they would have to administer more carefully. She too would have to make herself useful. The two Avaredos grinned strangely as they said these things, giving the impression that none of it was true, or that they found some pleasure in recounting them. They took away the pretty blue and pink dresses that the Marquis himself, in his infinite goodness, had trimmed down to her size when he had loved her, and they handed her a few kitchen rags. The window of the cellar, which had formerly been a very pleasant room where the Iguana loved to go and play, was boarded up, just as the Count had supposed, to remedy the lack of glazings; and the place was consigned to the beast while the room she had occupied before was destined to the use of guests. There had been no more sun nor sea nor morning nor evening for the little Iguana, but only an eternal twilight in which that last conversation with the person she referred to as "Daddy" constantly returned as a clearer and ever more terrible echo. But the worst had come when she had one day discovered a piece of broken mirror in the basement. Someone—Felipe to be precise—had left it there on purpose; and when the creature picked it up, she gazed with infinite stupor at her snout and her little green body. She was all green and ugly, nothing but a serpent, and Daddy, it was clear, had never said so out of kindness, or for some other reason she wouldn't have understood. But she did understand how greatly dissimilar she was to him and his family, and that going to paradise in a state like that was entirely out of the question. This thought, for a moment, was all her mind could deal with: that everything was over for her now and she'd no longer be going to paradise. Then, owing precisely to her lack of all power of reason, given her age and being an Iguana to boot, she broke into a giggle. This very moment was the beginning of what the masters of the household referred to as her "mischief."

Little by little, a kind of calm began to gather within the creature's death-like state; she no longer invoked the name from which all possible evil had spilled out over her, and all possible good as well; and as nature will have it in cases like these, she turned dull and spiteful. She soon had the habit of muttering ugly words beneath her breath at Hipolito whenever he scolded her for something badly done. Since she couldn't abide Felipe or the smirk with which he looked at her, she several times attempted to frighten him by emitting a particularly ugly lament from beneath a table or behind a door when the young man least expected it. She did everything wrong or sloppily, a little because it was really too much for her tiny paws, and a little for the sake of provocation. Her tongue grew so sharp that Felipe one day screamed at her and threatened to cut it out, and Hipolito began to call her a devil. Frightened not at all, the creature once distinguished by the name of "Estrellita" or "little star" reached the pits of vulgarity and informed the Marquis' kinsmen that she desired, for her labors, to be compensated in money, and not less than thirty *centavos* a month, which the brothers, after pretending to hesitate, agreed to give her in the form of certain flat stones that the Marquis himself collected, sometimes in tears, during his walks by the edge of the sea. You see why the little servant was so attached to them; she didn't fail, however, in her ignorance, to credit them with a certain pecuniary value as well.

This was how things had stood on the arrival, just about a month before Count Aleardo debarked at Ocaña, of the yacht of the lady who had been the involuntary cause of so many complications and who was now to depart with the Iguana's real treasure, which was of course her Daddy. From words caught here and there (the beast had developed the truly deplorable habit of eavesdropping), from certain great illuminations in the young man's face, and from certain victorious glances on the part of the Avaredos (who nevertheless made efforts to hide all events from her knowledge and shut her up at night in the hen house so that nothing would reach her ears), the creature had understood that her soul and therefore her very life was about to lift anchor and definitively to sail away, leaving her irreparably lost. The unpleasant attitudes she had assumed, her vulgarity, the ugly words, the slights, the cutting tongue, all the reactions of a stricken creature, but of a creature not yet finally deprived of hope, had all come suddenly to a halt. She seemed to have grown old and worn. The beast was truly incapable of holding herself up on her paws and had the strength to do nothing at all. Her mind continuously rumbled:

"Daddy's going away . . . going away . . . the sea. . . ."

She harbored no choler against the bride, since that sort of affection had nothing to do with her; and now, with no other hope than in moving the compassion of the heart she had so much loved, she accentuated her abjection, if such a thing is possible, with little dissimulations which we will find quite forgivable: for example, she would wrap a bandage around first one and then the other of her little paws (you see how the Count was taken in at the well!), or whenever her darling passed before her she would break into great wracking coughs that doubled her over; and more again of the same, but none of it, alas, was ever to any avail. The Marquis never noticed her, and the brothers showed no reaction except grumbling and laughter. It was only out of pure forgetfulness that the Marquis sometimes allowed her to remain in the room with the family as he read them some page from his writings. Everything was already finished for our diabolical little Iguana, and now, despite her doing her best to hold onto her calm, something was truly hurting her, and it hurt a great deal: she felt that some great rock had been levered onto her breast and everything inside of her wanted to scream:

"Daddy! Come and help me! My daddy has to come and help me!" but her voice no longer issued from her throat. It was precisely as though she were dead and the island uninhabited.

XVI

Daddo at the Cross-Roads

"Even the sea has an ending." Salvato's high spirits.

Waking up, she experienced a minute of nothingness, and then she remembered all these past events and what she had seen the previous night and that in the afternoon they would all depart. The silence was so immense as to make her think the night had not yet passed. But on growing accustomed to the darkness, the creature discerned a greying light descending from above through the opening that led to the kitchen, and she understood that the last day had begun. She broke into a fit of sobbing, yet it quickly abated. An image had come into her tiny cranium (we won't risk saying "an idea" since that was seldom, if ever, her case) and it gave her little bestial soul a strand of febrile hope. She stood up, her body stiff and pained, went to the corner where she kept her packets, collected them into a heap along with the coins Felipe's kick had spilled, and then she rapidly pouched everything together in a large red bandanna. She didn't forget the scarf she had received from the Count, nor the bitter fragment of mirror (since a woman, even the ugliest woman, is always attached to such an object), and all of it made for a voluminous bundle. Finally, she treated her head to a few passes of the comb, which she then put away in the pocket of her skirt. She covered her head with another kerchief, and holding both her breath and all the beats of her little green heart now at the point of bursting, she climbed back up (after quite a bit of careful listening) into the kitchen.

From here her goal was the meadow, all washed with a silver drizzle, and from there she intended to take both herself and her bundle to an elegant little dinghy with which we're already acquainted. She had a view to reaching a final destination of which we haven't been informed, but she was awaited by an ugly surprise.

Her shoulders were suddenly in the grip of hands as cold as snow, and an enormous dark figure stood shouting in front of her:

"Don't, for God's sake, give in to rage, don Ilario. That would be beneath you!"

"Daddy, Daddy," cried the little Iguana, recognizing her assailant to be her idol.

A veritable tempest of blows then pummelled down on her head, from the front, from the back, on the nape of her neck, on her snout, and the sky itself was screaming:

"Get her out of my sight or I shall kill her! My whole life is finished, and I owe it to this idiot, this stupid cretin! Ah, why didn't she die of scarlet fever like so many others? Why didn't her mother smother her in her diapers rather than wrap them around her buttocks? Whatever led me to take her in and feed her and dress her like the daughter of a nobleman? Now take that, you little thief, you wretched filth of a woman, you laziness. . . ."

You must not be surprised. Precisely this, in the intimacy of his family and when no one was there to observe him, was the language of our man of letters. And now in this hour of desperation don Fidenzio, who was present before him and whose arrival he had taken as a harbinger of misfortune and the breaking of his engagement, stood cancelled out of existence.

As for the creature, she had dropped the bundle and

tried for a while to defend herself, raising her little hands to protect her snout; but everything soon went dark all around her, and she tumbled over onto the grass, groaning a gruesome lament.

You are not to be saddened by these events. The poet of our lovely land tells us that everything passes away:

Even the sea has an ending.

With time, the pains of a little Iguana will likewise vanish. And you are not to grow indignant with the unhappy Marquis. He was overwhelmed by the fears that a young but nonetheless exhausted man can feel on seeing the emigration of his very last hope for a satisfying collocation in society. But we must also ask whether don Ilario's chances had been truly and definitively shattered. Or was it not, instead, that don Fidenzio had embarked for Ocaña at dawn solely for the purpose of rushing to inform the island noble that his mother-in-law had pardoned him? And couldn't the prelate's melancholy air be attributed, perhaps, to the failure of some machination he had pushed with too much energy?

This, Reader, is what we will shortly see, and what we most sincerely hope. But meanwhile we are not to forget the young Lombard architect, the not very intelligent son whom Countess Aleardi had sent to this corner of the earth on a mission of real estate speculation and who would seem to have forgotten his task, or at least to have given over most of his mind to thoughts of a different order. Bending over the oars of the *Luisina* in the scant light of the new day, he is rowing now towards the open sea, heedless of the subtle cold and the world's general gloominess.

As he boarded the *Luisina* and began to row off in the direction of the *Luisa,* the Count was in such a strange state of mind that he didn't even register surprise at smelling that characteristic odor of hot bread and coffee on the moist sea air. That was the typical smell of Milan at five o'clock in the morning, and there was even the screech of trams on their tracks. His whole soul had returned to the Lombard plain, or it was rather that the good, rich plain had caught up with him telepathically. On the one hand, he continued to hear the Captain's strong, almost joyful voice inside of him, and it showed him skies he had never seen before in his voyages as a man of high position; on the other hand, his love for his homeland was suddenly so strong it seemed to want to make him weep. "In just a few days I'll be back home again," he said to himself as though the phrase had gone to his head like wine (and surely no obstacle stood in the path of the traveller's natural plan to return to where he had come from); he could see himself as he opened the door to his studio and he envisioned his two dear secretaries as they smilingly advanced to greet him. Yet then he heard himself remark, "And what's that supposed to be all about? What am I going to do there? I'll just get old! Como, Bellaggio! A cruise every year; back to see friends in the fall! Adelchi! Walks down via Manzoni, thinking about the Islands! And meanwhile, in the Islands, innocents are destroying themselves and dying! They'll be calling out to me, but I won't be there. I *talk* about them. And this is my idea of a good and generous life! This is what I take as the way to serve my fellow men!" As clearly as in an antique print, via Bigli, the Count's beloved Piazza San Fedele, and all the green branchings of via Manzoni coalesced into an outline against the early morning clouds, and he felt a joy so strong that it hurt; but simultaneously he sensed a cry and an existential melancholy, as if everything within the region of his blood found it painful to abandon this place of so much misery, intrigue, and supplication. The most wrenching thing of all was the image of the Iguana that appeared before his eyes, appealing to him with a word that no one had ever spoken to him before and that seemed now to be the dearest, most beautiful word of all: "Daddy! Daddy!" It enchanted him, just like via Bigli or the Piazza, but maybe more. He didn't want to remember what he had heard Felipe's lips pronounce only shortly before about the beast's duplicity. Her condition spoke of death and dissolution and this, precisely, was what defined his obligation.

And now, arousing himself from this bewilderment, or rather perhaps as a consequence of this state of mind, he found himself certain that the *Luisa*, during the night, had drifted off to a greater distance—put it that way, and not that the island of Ocaña had drifted away from the boat, which would have been less probable. The distance was at least ten times greater than on the previous morning, and the Count was already irritated with Salvato and mulling on possible terms of reproof (which would also have given his mind some relief and helped to deliver it from attitudes of such sinister tenderness, and from such a plethora of thoroughly magical springtime impressions) when it further appeared that the *Luisa*'s shadow, cast on the sea with the help of a pale silver circle half-emerged from behind a column of pinkish-greyish smoke along the motionless horizon, and this circle was the sun . . . the *Luisa*'s shadow was far too large! His heart contracted, his mind had already reeled to the question of what was truly happening, and then he was once again in the midst of his state of sad calm, though now with a shading of surprise. He saw the *Luisa* where she ought to be and recognized that the rigging of another boat stood behind her—the Hopins' floating Venezuelan palace, which he had glimpsed the previous night at anchor in the cove. It stood there, quiet and still, and the easiest deduction was that the Hopins too—having decided for some reason to abbreviate their visit to Ocaña and give up hope of unravelling the secret that had brought them there—were also about to take their leave: whether with or without the Marquis was still to be ascertained.

He took this fact as a confirming sign of the imminence of his own departure, and it made him feel relieved, even despite the continuing presence of that new uncertainty provoked by the Captain's song.

He found Salvato in the hold, preparing a strong cup of coffee and showing a face marked with something unusually alive and gay. It gave the impression that the sailor had not been in any way bored during the absence of his skipper. Quite the contrary. He'd seem to have been furnished with pleasant distractions by the night that brought pain and despair to the Count. On being asked if anything was new, his reply was "all quiet." But he also shot a glance in the direcotion of the other yacht and gave the impression of waiting only to be questioned before releasing a cloud of revelations. The Count, however, paying no attention because of the way his own heart was closed, descended into his cabin where brass and wood furnishings were brightening palely in the smokey sunlight entering through the port-hole; and the first thing he did there was to fetch a pistol, in case complications should develop in perfecting the transaction. He then collected all the money he had on board, doing it up into the same kinds of packets he had seen the creature make. Three of them, two large, and one small. It amounted to six hundred thousand *pesetas* and two hundred and fifty thousand *escudos*, which was less than he had imagined, but he could write a few checks. While nervously searching through a drawer to see if he could find a few more coins, he also happened upon the emerald he had received from his mother; he immediately, happily picked it up and turned his thoughts to its possible recipients. The image of the person his heart had already chosen brought a bitter smile to his lips, and he inserted the emerald into the largest of the packages. This— if you're in any way surprised—was the least the Count could do to calm his apprehensions and his undefinable sense of remorse with respect to the creature he so greatly feared being forced to abandon. He could already imagine the *menina*'s amazement at the sight of real money and such a fantastic jewel, which he intended to present to her before weighing anchor. A faint smile made its way to his face, struggling against the obstacle of a tight cramp that simultaneously rose from his heart. It had lain there, fixed and rigid, ever since the night before.

He returned to the bridge looking for Salvato, to whom he wished to give his dispositions for departure, approximately two in the afternoon, and he found him while the sailor was exchanging greetings, in a low excited voice, with someone slouching carelessly from over the rail of the other boat. It was the Hopins' Negro maid. The two of them giggled with such crazy amusement that the youthful nobleman found himself for a moment with a thought that wounded him and that had never entered his mind before, or, if it had, it had left him indifferent: the two of them were making fun of his ingenuousness.

The sailor saw a sudden seriousness take hold in his companion's African eyes and turned about to discover a darkly frowning Count only two steps behind him; and at much the same moment, an entirely new and far from pleasant personage appeared beside the maid: a smallish man about fifty years old with a yellow if healthy face, black clothing, and a perfectly bald head. Seeing the Count, he doffed his hat—the gesture seemed almost facetious—and then stood there with his little beret in his right hand.

"*O senhor* Cole. . . ." and then, more directly to the Count, "I'm coming right away, sir." Salvato's words were just as clumsy as the rather approximate wave with which he took his leave of these two souls, and he then preceded the Count into the galley, where the coffee had boiled over onto the stove.

XVII
Salvato Knows

Where the sky closes in. Packing up.

"I see you haven't been bored . . . but that's nothing for me to complain about. . . . Thank you," said the Count, as Salvato, awkward and confused, served what was left of the coffee.

Self-controlled respect for the nobleman's pained withdrawal had taken considerable effort, and Salvato's attempts to maintain his composure and avoid all further offence now gave way to another burst of laughter, accompanied however by his certain knowledge of just how badly he would feel on finding himself dismissed (which he saw as clearly imminent). He therefore laughed with an apprehension, we might even say an anguish, that left the Count chagrined more than indignant. Moreover, wasn't that the sort of thing he himself had been known so often to do, going off into gales of laughter in the company of Adelchi for trifles so small as to amount to no reason at all? Indeed, he had the impression that his spirits had always been infinitely gay up until one o'clock on the previous afternoon. So he had nothing to say and cast his eyes to the floor and the sailor's feet.

"You can go ahead and fire me, sir," Salvato finally said, using the blue cuffs of his shirt sleeves to dry the copious tears that ran down his face. "I can't say you're being unfair, and I respect you for it. But try to understand. A man can't manage just a smile at what my ears have been listening to; all you can do is laugh till you laugh yourself to death."

Without even waiting for comment from the Count, almost in fact turning his back on him (by facing slightly to the porthole Salvato hoped his grins would cause no more grief), the sailor delivered a complete report, interrupted every now and then by a further guffaw, on what Ketty (the Hopins' domestic) had told him about the projected Segovia-Hopins matrimony. The project, he explained, was the work of don Fidenzio, and partly pivoted on the young man's title, partly on a long-standing friendship between the prelate and the young man's mother, who on her deathbed had begged the man of the cloth to try to take care of the boy; and it was obstructed, while at the same time intensely desired—a typically *parvenu* conflict—by no less than Mother Hopins, since it was common, broadly-rumored knowledge that the Marquis on his island had had, and continued still to the present, it seemed, to have a "flame." This "flame," unluckily, (the Count listened in attentive pain) was a little beast once dear to the young man's family, but a beast all the same and stupid as the devil to boot.

Apparently trying to defeat some even less containable outburst of laughter, Salvato couldn't help swallowing something back whenever he used the word "beast," and it seemed less a way of addressing reality than of euphemizing something deeper and utterly unnameable. The Count saw it, and had to brace himself against a wash of bitterness, almost expecting some truth previously hidden to him about the world to come swimming into view this morning from out of a theater of mimed obscenities. Passing a hand across his forehead, he suddenly lifted his tightly-drawn face:

"A beast—what do you mean by that?"

"I think the Count must know."

"But I don't."

At other moments the Count easily might have added, "Speak up." But now he was mortally tired and truly terrified of hearing any more. He had the confused impression that someone here was the victim of an abuse, and he vaguely suspected that he himself was one of its principle perpetrators. He was sweating even though the morning was cool and deathly still.

"It's not that this beast isn't really a beast . . . a beast just like all the rest of us, if you'll pardon my saying so, . . ."—the sailor had grown a little more earnest and his tone was a mixture of respect and embarrassment—"but in another sense as well, which is the serious part, and surely, sir, as a man of so much education. . . . I mean, to understand a thing like that . . ."

Salvato now broke off entirely, and the respect in his attitude had grown unconditional. The sailor had never realized before that a man of such wealth and esteem could have so limited a mind and a practically boyish squeamishness.

"Let's say I've heard enough. . . . We'll be weighing anchor at two in the afternoon, Salvato." The Count's reply had been a little while coming.

He stood up, gave a few instructions, and had again reached the bridge before turning around:

"That man, . . . *o senhor* Cole, was on the other boat? Or when did he get here? And what's he here for?"

"He got here, sir, about half an hour ago, with a boat of his own, from the coast. He's a theater agent, or something like that . . . but he buys and sells just about anything."

"And why didn't he go ashore?"

"First he had to wait until the Marquis was on ship. But now it's not sure the Marquis is coming aboard. . . . Even though. . . . What I say is that everything will get patched up. Don Fidenzio already rushed off to Ocaña as early as dawn. He looked desperate."

144

"But why should he be desperate," the Count distractedly queried.

"Well, just between us, and to pass on what I've heard, it's that don Fidenzio wants to buy the island himself and turn it into a meditation center, or a luxury relaxation resort. But the island has really grown on Miss Hopins, and so the priest has been trying to get his way by putting pressure on the mother's superstitions. But after what happened last night, the marriage risks calling off, and the priest seems scared. . . . He wants it both ways, having the cake and eating it too . . . not of course that this is what he says out loud. So now he's talking up a storm with the little lord of the island, and this poor *senhor* Cole doesn't know what to do. . . ."

"He doesn't know what to do . . ." repeated the Count, after listening deafly. He had already set his foot on the ladder when he turned around and gave still more instructions, distractedly, while observing the other boat. The lovely creature he had seen the night before as she was visiting the cellar had appeared on the high, gilded bridge and was fixing him with the intelligent, self-assured smile of her gracious face, not improbably expecting, having been informed of his presence by the maid, that he'd come to present himself and ask to speak with her.

But precisely this delicious apparition in the grey-gold light of the new day suddenly revealed to the Count that a meeting (to which he might have been favorable but a few minutes earlier) was absolutely useless. His intuition seemed to flash, and he saw that this young woman—aside from her economic potency, created on the ruin of the Guzmans and now, with the marriage, about to restore them once again to grace—was exactly what was needed to bring the Marquis' disturbed, blighted mind back to health; and that don Ilario Segovia —even lacking a marriage that gave him repossession of his mother's goods and therefore relieved him of all need of assistance—would never, even in poverty, have profited more by Milan than by the companionship of this strong young woman. His destiny had never lain nor would ever lie in literature, but rather in a modern, well-equipped farm and the joys of a husband and land-holder. He could see the marriage would take place, and Ocaña would be ceded to the far-sighted archbishop so as to relieve the bride and groom of all misgivings. The only thing that wasn't clear to him, unless he himself took care of it, and quickly, was the case of the ill-starred daughter of the place, the have-not Iguana, for whom there was no apparent destiny.

"I think now...excuse me...a slight delay..." he said, struggling against the stutter we've seen as typical of his hours of trial, directing his words to Salvato.

And Salvato—who was later very much surprised by what he had said—replied almost as if in pain, and as if the boat had many years since lain in port with the Count at some enormous distance away:

"God...God bless you, sir. You've been like a father to me. And...thank you for everything!"

"But not at all, my dear," responded the Count in his habitually courteous way, but virtually without expression, as he descended into the *Luisina*. A melancholic gravity rose over his face and remained there.

The sea and sky, moreover, after the sun's vain first attempt to take charge of the firmament, had likewise sealed over and grown profoundly melancholic.

Never again—if ever again he were able to think about something other than the island of Ocaña and if his mind were to recall the existence of calendars—would the Count be able to believe that spring had been bursting forth behind that sky and that sea, so still and lifeless. Rather than spring, he'd

have thought of some first autumnal peace, when the confla-
gration of the sky has disappeared in the course of a night,
after a great glowing lustrousness of the moon, and the following day is cold and dark. No matter that today, in fact, was
anything other than cold and dark; really quite the contrary.
It still had that sharpness of breath of after the first rains, and
that sky more similar to a theater scrim when the actors have
all gone home than to any vault of air. Thousands of forms,
their predominant tone a grey or yellow mixed with the color
of turtle doves and a few flourishes of green, hung down from
the hooks of the sky like old lace dresses tattered by time and
some evil that had afflicted their proprietress. In the sea,
contrarily, no light at all, except a leaden reflection towards
the distant horizon. Closer to shore, where the Count rowed
his boat, it was brown as earth. The oars pulled hard to enter
and leave the water and shone dully on coming up free into
the air. The atmosphere's obscurity, that yellowness, reflected from the wet wood. The island, as the boat approached, looked completely uninhabited, except that the
oaks, ruffled by an invisible wind, had turned from red to
black, and then, in patches, were red again. They might have
been on fire.

Voices from people he couldn't see came from behind a
rise along the beach and then mingled with a vulgar song.
Their tone, less happy than shameless, contrasted strangely
with the sweet, noble agony of the earth and sky. The
Avaredo brothers. A few moments later the Count caught
sight of them, intently tying lengths of rope around a piece of
furniture, small as a match box against the immense horizon.
A tall thin door, adorned with a long narrow mirror that reflected a slanting sea, revealed it to be a wardrobe. Four
chairs and the dining-room table, lashed together with
cords, already stood on the beach beneath the oak trees. The
mirror, showing the sea and the sky, the one dark as iron, the

other pale, appeared to open back onto a great light, which made the Count feel suddenly serene:

"They're . . .they're leaving; so everything has been straightened out," the young man remarked to himself.

What, precisely, had been straightened out would not have been easy to define from any strictly logical point of view; but the Count, that morning, as we've noticed, was quite distracted and behaved like someone who was arriving at every moment from across great distances, as the sea does.

When his boat passed in front of the Avaredo brothers, he didn't see them and was not seen. He stepped ashore from the *Luisina*, pulled up the boat into a shallow tidal pool, and set out over the beach towards the house.

Standing before the building and raising his eyes to the tower that held the library, he deduced from a flickering light in the chamber that the Marquis would be busy recopying or correcting his manuscripts and didn't want to be disturbed. So the first thing to do, he decided, was to go to the kitchen and seek out the Iguana, from whom he hoped to receive an explanation of the mystery so clear to everyone but himself; he also wanted to form an idea of what the little servant would prefer to do: to depart for Milan early in the afternoon (what he himself most desired), or to have him remain at her service on the island. Manrique's song had just so strong an effect on the nobleman's heart. But in the kitchen the Iguana was nowhere to be seen. The breakfast cups and plates still dirty in the sink convicted the little servant, probably prey to some suspicion, of not having done her chores, and he imagined she must have gone off offended and worried and closed herself up in her room. He therefore went to the hatch, lifted the door, and descended the stairs, but only to find that the movements of his flashlight beam were answered by greater, more miserable disorder than usual. It was frightening too that the bags she used as a pallet at the back of the room had been removed and lay in a heap beneath the stairs, much as mattresses and sheets are stripped way and set aside when someone dies. Even the Iguana's money, two bags full lay at the foot of the stairs, to the side of a bandanna in which it must have been wrapped. Like a burden suddenly too difficult to deal with, it apparently had been thrown down through the opening above. This was a sign of nothing good. For the bed to have been removed and the creature's savings still to have been left behind could mean that the order to dislodge had come so swiftly she hadn't been able to collect her goods.

The Count was depressed and full of self-blame for having lost so much time with so many vain words, and his new apprehensions made him timid in spite of her being dear to him. He wanted to call out to her, but he was also afraid. Finally he yelled:

"Iguana! Iguana!"

XVIII
A Strange Iguana

The colloquy. "The Virgin won't allow it." In the hall.

He received no reply, except that after a moment a muffled noise seemed to come from above, down through the
other hatchway in the closet of his own room: the same high-
pitched whimper, *nao nao*, that had sliced into his mind the
day before. He climbed the ladder, groped his way out of the
closet, and discovered his intuition not to have failed him.

Unexpectedly calm and unafraid, she stood before his
eyes. With a kerchief wrapped around her head and several
times around her neck, she was dragging a huge grey broom
distractedly about the guest room. Rather than cleaning she
might have been scattering dust and disorder out of spite. Her
small dry eyes, moreover, seemed oddly fixed and unrespon-
sive.

The Count's first impulse was to approach her and take
her in his arms, telling her what he intended to do for her and
that starting right now she was forever to think of him as her
servant and her daddy and she'd bear his name and have all
of his money; but then he looked at her better, and something
held him back. He suspected—from the out-sized kerchief,
her general listlessness, that way of dragging the broom,
vexatiously making a mess rather than cleaning—that the
creature was scheming to gain by subterfuge what he spon-
taneously wanted to give her; she was deliberately playing on

his feelings. At any other time he would have laughed, but now (though not without a thought to her future re-education and how best to lift her up from such a sad state of corruption), he went rigid and drew himself tall:

"Look there, you're only scattering dust about," he began. "Who could have possibly have taught you to sweep up like that? It would be better not to do it at all." His voice had managed to turn cold and impersonal, whereas the attitude in his eyes was curiously timid.

The Iguana, as tired servants or irritated children will often do, pretended not to have heard him and continued in her hesitant, disorderly way to push the dust about on the floor from one place to another. At that point the Count indeed approached her and took the broom from her hands; in fact, he literally cast it away, telling her with a tremor in his voice that she was never again to touch such a thing. Then— since her steady, will-less gaze was simply more than he could stand and he wanted to make up with her—he took her by a shoulder and guided her over to the table, where he put down his packets of authentic money and opened the largest, which was the one that held the emerald. The eyes of the beast immediately flared with a sparkle and a softening that just as quickly disappeared, but not before the Count had understood that she wasn't totally unacquainted with the value of money. This too was something of which he would have to heal her. Now, however, he wanted to see her smile.

"Go ahead and touch it," he said, prodding her hand a little with his own, and again surprised that her skin was so cold.

"This belongs to me?" asked the Iguana.

"But of course."

"The stone too?"

"Everything."

After a brief hesitation, she cupped her hands, picked

151

up all the money, and slipped the "gift" into a ragged pocket of her apron. But she didn't bubble over as on the previous morning into that *"thank you ... thank you!"* that *"nao para mim ... nao para mim ..."* which had filled the count with such a sweet sense of joy. This time it might have seemed that he had given her a handful of sand.

"Are you happy? With this you'll be able to go out and buy yourself..."

What kept him from continuing was a movement with which the creature inadvertently dislodged her scarf; it loosened and opened and the Count saw several ugly marks on her thin dirty neck. Such a detail, along with her dreamy, exhausted air made him think that something truly serious had taken place in his absence. Hastily putting the other package down (which he had already unwrapped), he reached out to turn the creature's head with his hand, but she instantly drew back from his touch. She winced in pain, or expected pain, and one of her eyes twitched shut while the other stared up in alarm, yet not really at him.

"What has happened to you? Why don't you tell me? Have you gone out and hurt yourself?" Aleardo anxiously demanded.

No reply. Then:

"I have a cold, *o senhor*," with her obvious mendacity belied only by the statement's utter vacuity, so typical of how children up to a certain age can be oblivious to all sense of the ridiculous.

"Iguana," said the Count (his eyes showed a touch of bitterness, or even supplication, and he didn't want to address her by name since her name somehow embarrassed him), "why must you always lie like that? Why...." Then he stopped, incapable of continuing. The question that had formed in his mind was: "Why must you act like such a little

152

devil?" His intimate core of passionate sadness refused to allow the expression of this metaphysical lament, and no such phrase, in fact, was ever to cross his mind again. He maintained his silence and watched the sea through the framing of the window; it struck him as growing even more mute. Then, weakly:

"Tell me: would you come away with me?"

"Where . . . *o senhor?*"

"The Marquis and I have made an agreement," said the Count, feeling no remorse for the lie (the second he had ever told in his life) since he hoped to be rewarded with seeing the little servant smile, "and I'm to take you away with me today, when I leave at two o'clock. You will never be a servant again. I'll be the servant, and I'll be serving you. Can you understand that?" Additional words refused to come—owing to some inexplicable mystery the scene contained—and his eyes blurred with tears. Lowering his head, he caught a glimpse of the beast from some bottomless profundity: she was observing him, quite steadily, with the very same gaze— intense and grave, estranged and unruffled—that had struck him the previous night in the chicken coop. It was as though her mind had focused on something of supreme importance, but something concerned with a wholly different subject—a subject she refused to mention out of pride, or that rankled against some infantile resentment. So she simply maintained silence and let her eyes examine the face of this gentleman who wanted to be her friend. Finally:

"Do I have to go to hell?"

"What did you say?" Aleardo hadn't understood.

"I said, do I have to go to hell, I mean when I die, *o senhor?*"

"Neither to hell nor to heaven," replied the Count, suddenly cool since he felt the duty to open a serious discussion

153

of the creature's condition, "if you don't have a soul."

Another silence, with the Iguana slightly turning her neck, wary of a returning pain.

"The Marquis," she continued, her voice so thin as to seem to have fissured (and at any moment likely to fall into shards) "is going to heaven today, right after lunch. He's going on the boat; and after all the water, there's the sky and the Holy Virgin, and all the constellations. But I can't go there. The Virgin won't allow it."

"The Virgin! What you mean is America!" This bitter reply would surely have sprung from his lips if he hadn't seen sudden reason to hold his peace. The Iguana's eye was assuming an ever stranger aspect (and we say eye in the singular since only one of her orbs, the left one—the other was closed—looked up at him), revealing the white around the pupil with a sort of terrible intensity. And that word "constellations," coming from a creature who certainly couldn't be suspected of ever having read it! It reminded the Count of the manuscript dedication he had chanced to discover, and it thus reopened in his mind a passage he had already shut up. The word spread a lightning glare of illumination over expanses of dizzying obscurity and then reconsigned the Count to the dark and an even more acrid sadness.

He felt that the whole world of Christianity had cracked in two and was precipitating into the abyss. His pain was enormous and he asked, "Who . . . told you that?"

Here again, the creature slightly stretched her neck, wanting to focus it as the site of all her hurts. Seeing something utterly unpretty in that movement and in the way the creature's gaze remained unreal, the Count needed all the more to find an exit from so much uncertainty. This time he begged:

"Who . . .who told you that, little Iguana?"

Her only reply was the sweet, stupid stare of a creature

154

resigned to the uselessness of formulating further noises or bothering to babble them out; still twisting her neck, and seeming to find the pain truly troublesome, she slipped into total estrangement. Forgetting the emerald among the trash, and the broom on the floor, she turned and left the room.

That mysterious instinct of the outcast may have advised her of the Marquis' approach. This, at any rate, is what the Count imagined as he himself stepped out into the corridor to see where the little servant, so thoroughly disturbed, had gone, and instead saw don Ilario descending the stairs from the library. The poet held a copy of his manuscripts in his hand and smiled while still looking sad.

Behind him, in the light of the great window, was the black outline of don Fidenzio; and the two of them, coming down from the tower after a long and serious discussion, surely had never expected to encounter the Count in the hall. The haggard Marquis accentuated his smile, at the same time pressing his lips more tightly together, and the Archbishop seemed some huge dark moth transfixed by fear at the sight of an approaching hand. As if attempting to mimeticize with the first available place of shelter, the prelate pressed himself back against the glassy expense of the window and appeared to hope to vanish among those other figures at his back, those portraits of Portuguese kings. Neither Ilario nor don Fidenzio had caught any inkling of Aleardo's state of mind: the Count was like a person who has just begun to listen to the movement of the sea, and who can hear nothing else.

He remained in fact (the Count) with his back against the wall, his eyes towards the boy who now approached him. Yet really he was looking at nothing. His mind was just that thick with sadness. The words the poet spoke seemed so many scraps of printed paper.

Don Ilario graciously opened as though no serious dialog had ever taken place between them and they had only banalized their time in idle conversation:

"Hello, Daddo, how are things going? I disappeared for the whole morning, but you'll have no trouble guessing why. Have a look at this." He held out the manuscripts of *Portugal* and *Penosa*, flipping them open at random to give a rapid glance at all his minute corrections. He also proffered a letter enclosed in a yellow envelope, which was the authorization for the Count to act on the young man's behalf in his dealings with the publisher in Milan.

The Count took the manuscripts, automatically, an imperceptible tremor moving his hand, and then begged to be allowed to leave them aside for a moment since he had to make a request and would need all of the Marquis' courteous attention. His voice spoke in a whisper, and his handsome face was a scene of obscurity and confusion.

"I don't understand," replied Ilario, observing the Count with curiosity and with what the Count himself experienced as a touch of chilliness, almost of disappointment. "But in any case, certainly not here, and my studio won't do either since it's rather in disorder. Better to go to the dining room." A brief glance at don Fidenzio asked the prelate for a moment to take his leave—as if the Count's very existence didn't need to be acknowledged—and the Marquis showed his guest towards a completely empty room. Everything had been removed by his brothers.

XIX
The Terrible Mendes

A question for the unions. Absurd! Confusion.

The bareness of the dining room, now totally devoid of furniture, evoked not a single word of explanation even after the two young men had entered the chamber, and the Marquis betrayed no whit of embarrassment for the lack of anywhere to take a seat. His bearing contained some new directness that must have stemmed from his colloquy with the priest and then been driven, as it were, out of latency by the indiscretion moiling forward from the Count's anxiety. Or perhaps the talk had furnished the Marquis with reasons for imperturbable self-assurance, which is a vigorous cast of mind propending not necessarily to what we'd call disdain, but surely it encourages a lack of regard for the opinions that others may form of our behavior. Such a warmth of vigor might now have been expanding within a sense of having shed some intimate burden, and the Marquis' attitude to the Lombard—the bosom friend of just shortly before—allowed itself a register of unspeakable superficiality and even of unconcealed impatience.

With an intonation that froze the heart of the poor young Count, the Marquis spoke the words, "And what, my dear, did you want to say? I'm all ears."

Two hours earlier on the beach, as he clutched his

friend by the hand, the Count could never have imagined that his feelings for the Marquis might dissolve from one moment to the next like a handful of foam and leave nothing in their place except the absurd desperation of a haggard old servant. But he still had the gift of the very same eyes, limpid and melancholy, that had conquered Ilario and comforted Estrellita, and they were staring now at the face of a total stranger. He had to do justice to the facts. This man now standing before him was no longer the tremulous Ilario, but the hard and determined Mendes: that gorgeous, self-confident youth who had appeared the night before on the balcony. The Lombard's mind twitched with weakness and vacillation. Unable to rediscover the sensitive boy, the quivering soul of the Orphan of Ocaña, and confronted instead with a tough-minded man of the world, the Count had to make an admission: he had no previous experience of such mutations and metamorphoses and was therefore at their mercy, helpless in the face of their horror. He could guess at no ability that might come to his rescue, since he had remained unschooled in real scientific knowledge, which would offer some explanation for these psychic phenomena and transfers of the ego. So his only possible reaction to this precipitation of events was a buckling of something inside of him, and a wave of that faintness of the poor in spirit for whom no earth is *terra firma* and whom no hand promises to approach, if not to deliver a cuff about the ears.

Yet some corner of his being still remained superior to the reach of universal horror, no matter how slightly or with how great a sense of misery. It was a question of time. He was exhausted, overwhelmed, and lost within a cloud of black discoveries, and his ear had much to listen through before once again discerning the voice that had ordered him to come to Ocaña, just as it had always ordered him to follow the path of justice. No straits in which he found himself could make a difference. So while the smile of this man Mendes began dangerously to shift, deforming itself into open impatience (now it was truly Mendes, and no one else), the Count allowed his eyes to rove beyond the glass of the window and survey the breaking swells of the sea. He finally spoke:

"First of all, my dear, please forgive me if I allowed myself to make you the object of a display of friendship during our conversation *of some years back*. You'll believe me, I hope, to have acted in accordance with feelings that were perfectly sincere, and I would never willingly have given offense. No such intention was ever so much as remotely present in my mind, and you can give me credit for that, even if I have nothing, at the moment, with which to settle the debt."

These words might have been more than obvious, and Mendes took no notice of the Count's outlandish and pitiful error concerning the amount of time elapsed. (Barely more than a few hours!) He replied, the vaguest of smiles on his lips:

"Let's now, if you have no objection, get to the point."

"There's the question, then, of your people. . . ."

This is what the Count was reduced to by his desperate inability to face the subject of the creature, and especially with this powerful, lordly personage. Simply to mention her, not of course to himself but to her masters, was enough to fill him with anguish, and his very sense of self-preservation had led him to speak of the Marquis' "people" (which meant nothing at all) rather than of his beast or servant, which is what she really was.

Fortunately, the young man understood.

"You're referring . . . to the little beast?"

"Yes . . ." replied the Count, his forehead pearling over with sweat. One can't quite say how the Marquis achieved such an effect—if perhaps it didn't lie in keeping his face composed into a certain strange smile and continuing to nibble at his fingernails while his interlocutor floundered into ever greater suffering—but the Count was feeling himself go cold, and obscurity was mounting inside of him, as though he were about to faint.

"Has something," he continued, after waiting in vain for some hint of encouragement (the slightest nod would have helped to mollify his anguish), " . . . has something, my dear, brought about a change in your relationship with the very soul of this island, by which I mean to refer to your servant . . . that relationship that was once so fine and friendly with your dear little pet? Some transgression you can't forgive her? I dare to ask, and even—if you'll permit—to insist, since I have the feeling that your departure is not only imminent, but definitive as well, eternal, and I'd like to look after her and help her to grow and again to flower; but I can see she has gone astray in some long-gone promise you made to her, and now she refuses to have the will to live and she's starting to die."

He had expected an explosion of rage, but it hadn't come. He heard only the sound he had listened to before, clearly the thud of the surf on the beach; and in a luminosity more yellow than livid now pervading the air of the dark room, he saw Mendes' face go drawn and thin, if only for an instant. The space of a single sad beat of his golden eyelashes. The Count imagined that this might be a hopeful sign for the creature so dear to him, but he was wrong: the attitude that next took charge of Mendes' face was a nameless rigidity. Looking up at the Count from lovely blue eyes showing only indifference and gloomy curiosity, the Marquis queried:

"You . . . you've spoken with her?"

"Yes . . ."

"I see," the Marquis replied, assuming a reflective air. "There has been a slight misunderstanding, and I can explain it in just a few words. It derives from an erroneous interpretation of the function of the trade unions. These unions, as you know, have established the payment of a tax in favor of one's servants, to take care of their needs in old age, or, lacking that, a simple wage increase. Somehow or another, she heard talk of this and asked, if not for social security, then for a raise. She failed, however, to consider that she had never become a member of a union. So, for the time being, it hasn't been possible to give her satisfaction. That's all there is to it."

There was a long moment of silence in which the thudding thunder of the surf was replaced by the wind. A flock of the dead was in flight from one side of the island to the other, pursued by a legion of demons who pushed and prodded them with sharpened sticks, as herdsmen handle cattle. Passing before the house, they wailed a message for the sick-hearted Count: "Careful! Careful!" Feeling it all to be too much for him, this gentleman stood staring at Mendes with the very same gaze, severe and yet full of supplication, that typically distinguished the Iguana: he was begging and demanding that the Marquis make a choice between truth and mendacity, sanity and alienation; that he choose non-alienation even at the cost of his life.

"No. . . . That's not what she talked to me about. . . . Her complaint had nothing to do with that."

"No? And what then, if you'll be kind enough to say, would it be?"

"She has given me to understand—and please don't be angry to hear it, my dear, since you must try to understand her—but there was a time, some previous time in your friendship, of which I admit I know nothing at all, when she tells me you promised to take her on a journey to Heaven . . . and that later you were no longer so disposed.

The Marquis' head snapped up as if he had been bitten by a snake. But he wasn't aghast. He was very attentive, almost bathed in a light of blank desperation.

"I would have made such a promise? Did she really tell you that?"

He didn't, however, wait for an answer. Clasping his hands and twisting his intertwined fingers with a force that ought to have broken them, he stepped back away from the Lombard and began pacing up and down across the room. Seemingly witless, but still with a savage edge of irony, he continually repeated:

"Incredible! Shocking! Madness!"

Then, in a kind of deranged incredulity:

"To Heaven! So that's the pass we've come to!"

The Count was in tears.

"Don't cry, Daddo," said Mendes, striding back in his direction and halting directly in front of him. Rage, nobility, the greatness of his ancestry, and who knows what else, were turning the Marquis into a creature of astonishing beauty. His clothes—the identical clothes in which the Count had seen him on first landing on the island—assumed a vivid splendor, as though replaced by others, and were virtually aflame. Everything about him was beautiful, virile, new, and the winds of hope—the most sublime of hopes—appeared to fill that youthful sail. Almost bobbing like a boat scudding before a southwest wind on the turquoise sea, he added. "In any case, she's no longer here."

A knock sounded at the door, and in reply to Mendes' harsh "Come in," Felipe and Hipolito stepped into view. They too wafted a manner of something rich and new, which was quite a strange contrast to the sack full of stones (that's what it seemed to be) that they carried—a sad, miserable package suspended between them. Despite its writhing, it seemed destined to be thrown into the sea.

"The Archbishop wants a word with you," whispered

Felipe. He might have been mistaken, but the Count peered out from the depths of his suffering—which was increasingly accompanied by feverish lucidity and a heavy sensation of weakness—and was convinced that both of the brothers had glanced momentarily at the sack, not perhaps with compassion, but with remembrance and commiseration while still altering nothing in their souls. The Count's soul filled with suffocation and the certainty of standing before a crime.

"Surely you won't allow . . . money . . . listen . . . I'll go straight away to get it." The words, as he vacillated, tried to make their way past lips once again afflicted by that ridiculous stuttering typical of the moments when the Count was beside himself. But neither Mendes nor those other gentlemen appeared to listen. Some great agitation raged about the walls of the house, and it wasn't a question, or not only a question, of the tempest now taking possession of the sea. The Count could hear shouts, or screams, and to some degree he believed it the voice of the servant rebelling against the bitterness of her fate. Then, but this was surely impossible, it was a chorus of Yankee voices—those strident voices from the night—broadcast from a bullhorn and ordering the Marquis to come and join them. An all-containing chaos: laments and tears, laughter and proud self-assurance, the supplications of the past and the commands of the future. There was likewise the spirit of nature, and then nature herself amidst all the justice of her choler. But one fact was more factual than any other: the architect's overtaxed mind was in delirium.

He managed nonetheless to discern these words, in which reality and symbol were desperately, unfortunately intermingled, as in avant-garde novels. They made his blood run cold:

THE COOK: "By now the weather has broken. The swells are cresting and breaking, and the Hopins have decided to sail immediately. So hurry up, everybody is waiting for your final instructions."

MENDES: (irritated): "You mean you're incapable of taking care of things without me? Can't you see I'm talking with this gentleman?"

FELIPE: "You call him a gentleman?"

MENDES: "Segovia was here until just a few minutes ago, out in the corridor. Haven't you seen him? Isn't he already aboard?"

COLE (surprised): "Aboard what, sir? Stand back away from that well! You could fall!"

XX

Daddo at the Well

The pretty little girl. Armed! On the trail of the culprits.

The scene in fact had changed, and the Count, if only for a moment, could formulate the thought that things had returned to normalcy, now worth more to him than ever before. Despite the torment in his mind, he found himself surrounded once again by the grey diffuseness of the morning air. He saw the sky, felt the pure, gusty ocean breeze, and briefly imagined he was still the same man he had always been, the Aleardo who had debarked on this melancholy island the day before. Rather than Mendes, the good Ilario stood beside him, reassuringly attired in his modest daytime clothes. Likewise for the dark and squalid brothers, and that nice little man called Cole. But they all bent forwards around the well, and something in their tense excited faces made the Count feel sick. He suddenly knew his life was over: that he would never return to Milan or board his boat or contemplate the blue of the sea; never again see Palos or other ports of call, nor sail into the Gulf of Genoa, nor walk down his much-loved via Bigli. None of that was any longer possible, because the Iguana was dead.

He peered down into the well and saw her, or thought he saw her, some sixty feet below: a creature of exceptional beauty, dressed in a white lace dress, a pink sash for a belt, and two small pink shoes. She slumped forward over her knees at the bottom of the well, motionless as in sleep, her position the same as when he had watched her during the night in the cellar, after everyone else had gone.

"But she's alive!" he cried; and then, mixing pain and surprise, "It's someone else!"

Looking more sharply, he saw nothing at all. "According to me, she's no longer there," said Ilario, having paid the Count no attention. His face was red, his cheeks scalded by tears, and it was clear just how dear the creature had been to him, basically. He stepped back from the well.

"There's water at the bottom, *o senhor marques*," said Cole. "Not very much, but enough to cover a body."

The three men moved a short distance away. Only Cole remained beside the well, except of course for the Count, who was perhaps in the grips of fever. He continued to stare at the bottom of the hole and to see something that made him weep: that delectable, luckless little figure. Now it also had a hand, motioning five dark fingers to signal that she had lain there for five full years—five years in excruciating suffering.

"Iguana," cried the Count, his pain now peaking towards madness. A rope hung down from the scaffolding above the well, not a very long rope; still, it might be enough and he resolved to descend. But on clambering up onto the edge of the well, he felt deceived. He changed his mind and returned into the room.

As the Count's right hand pulled the collar of his jacket yet higher around his face (the downpour of rain in the room was torrential and accompanied by claps of thunder), the scene of shortly before resumed. Something about it must have been wrong, and the secret author of the passions that govern (or destroy) the world had dispersed it, cleansing it of flourishes and hesitations that obscure the clarity of human vision and block the advancing hegemony of justice. Ilario—

166

dressed as when he had first greeted the Count, yet nonetheless all new, well-groomed, and perfumed—once again descended the stairs from the tower library, and a limpid ray of light, reflected entirely for his benefit from the window panes, formed a halo around his head. In one hand a scroll of freshly copied papers, tied together with a yellow ribbon; and behind him—just as in the previous scene—the black don Fidenzio, laughing some pleasantry into the poet's ear. But the heads within that gorgeous splash of sunlight rayed no greetings towards the Count when they turned barely enough to appraise him with a sidelong glance. Tired and searching for shelter from the wet raging tempest, Aleardo pressed back against the wall. The gentlemen on the stairs drew faces unceremoniously expressive of their feelings and remained unaware of how much the Count had changed. They regarded him with pique and open displeasure.

"But my dear Count, you have gone entirely mad!" the young man shouted, more or less with the voice of the wind. "To enter my house with such filth! What must have come over you?"

The home of the Marquis of Segovia—we've described its woeful conditions—had undergone a most profound mutation: polished and splendid, it was the family mansion of the Hopins, because time had passed, the Hopins had a title, and they were great patricians in far-away America.

The thread of a voice in Aleardo's throat caught like a kind of dry unrecognizable wail, in which surely you'd have found no trace of the hallmarks of his Lombard renown: his gaiety, serenity, coolness, and impervious immutability. He retorted:

"It's a question of justice. So you will have to excuse me."

"I'll be with you in an instant."

Subdued, the Portuguese noble offered this reply and

entrusted his papers to the prelate (who stopped for a moment to study them) before agilely descending the crimson runner down the center of a stairway apparently made of gold. Reaching the corridor where the Count stood waiting, he took his friend by the hands and addressed him in tones of sincere and natural concern.

"But you're ill. You're trembling. What has happened to you, Daddo?" Then he sank into a desolate voice that made the Count wince. "But you're armed!"

The weapon slipped automatically back into its holster and the Count attempted to smile. His face was livid.

"No . . ." he stated, "this isn't what you have to fear . . ." his forehead furrowing from the gentle exertion of staying abreast of things. From time to time he had to make an effort. It was difficult to remember so many shiftings, just as it was difficult to see them in the first place, difficult to make distinctions within these continuous superimpositions of the real and the unreal. " . . . not this, Ilario, but your very own soul, as I fear mine. There is something we're totally ignorant of, something we refuse to know, someone hidden who closes our eyes. . . . There's a deception working to the harm of people who are weaker than we are. . . . Something in our education, in our way of seeing the world, some fundamental error that calls down calamity on a great number of people, and that's what I want to strike against."

He sat down on a bench. It had just appeared, and the Marquis held out a glass of water to him. Ilario looked at the Count with infinite pity.

"Understand! But on the basis, Daddo, of what? You're to stand aside for the Constellations. They've come to gather the Holy Body! God is dead! is dead! God is dead!"

These words were followed by a sudden outburst of tears and then by a savage ringing of bells—an hosanna or a death knell, one couldn't tell which—but what Ilario had said left the Count indifferent. Aleardo had changed and had come to feel that the truly horrid side of life lay in compassion. It offered evil a chance to veil its crimes, and goodness opened a portal to profoundest weakness. Out of the cloud which had been his life, he now could cull no other purpose than the rebirth of God. His liberation from the sepulchre, and the restoration of Rightness. For the Iguana, as for every other fact of life, he no longer had any thoughts at all.

The need for air had been a torment for quite some time, so he walked to the window. Looking out, he saw a group of people passing towards the left side of the house, following the path to the well. Ilario headed the group, crying, and directly behind him came a girl the Count had never seen before, all grey and barefoot, and dragging a large bucket. The Hopins were there as well, Mr. and Mrs., their manner worried and concerned.

"So first they murdered Him, with their arrogance and lust for power, and now they intend to recover the corpse, as if that served some purpose!" Speaking with such an excess of sarcasm, even to himself, was something to which the Count was unaccustomed.

Nor was he accustomed to the face reflected on the window pane. The eyes contained enormous emptiness, and the forehead showed something arch and fantastical, quite alien to the Count's mild physiognomy; and the agued lips moved imperceptibly, issuing no words.

He could feel no love for such a face, so he turned and left the room. The hearing, moreover, would begin before too long and was sure to offer amusement. The Hopins would carry God's corpse into the court room, claiming He was dead, and one had to resign oneself, and He was now at the beginning of a new and different plane of existence. But the Count would make it understood that none of this was true.

A path had opened within the wall, and where the tempest had raged it now rained softly. Very softly, like crying. The world was green, despite its being November, and nothing showed traces of the recent tumult. He would have liked to go to the well, which he was sure was only a short walk away. Instead he descended. He slowly went downwards. *Downwards* was where the audience was held. It was difficult to breathe.

The Count's real location in this frangent of time, whether at the well along with the others, to see if there was any vestige of the Body of God, or wandering about the island with the pistol in his hand on the trail of the culprits, or at the bottom of the well, or in that cold hallucinated court room, is something, Reader, though it may strike you as strange, that we are unable to tell you. If you're inclined to petition for an explanation of these continuous passages from one place to another, changes of scene, broken dialogs and rapidly telescoping locales, if you want to know the truth of these interplays of houses, winds, and wells, of trembling paths and mute interiors, of living leaves and dead walls, of sunrays and lamplights, of progress and stasis, of immobility and movement, and above all of a waxing pain, of a sadness knowing no repose, of unspeakable anger intermixed with commonplace words, and as well of the disappearance of both our Iguana and those prodigies and peals of laughter that have characterized our story up to now, in that case you ought to reflect—while awaiting whatever explanations we yet may prove able to furnish (presuming the very existence of explainability within this world of inscrutable phenomena where you too make your home)—you should reflect, thoughtful Reader, on the particularly narrow mind of our young Lombard architect and on how it nonetheless harbored a generosity of which he had never been aware previous to debarking on this tragic island. You yourself are safe, and can turn the tranquil light of reason onto the tremendous truth of the soul: on its being here, everywhere, and nowhere, and all while a strong young body walks now in one direction, now in another, carried along whatever paths it travels by whatever new questions may arise within the mind it encloses. And what is a body when compared to the spirit that guides it and to which that body, those hands, and those eyes have but the simple duty of furnishing expression? And what is time, the time in which such thoughts and actions find articulation? And what is space, if not ingenuous convention? And what is an island, or a city, the world itself with its multitudinous capitals, if not simply a theater where the heart, stricken by remorse, can pose its ardent questionings? So you mustn't, Reader, be amazed if the sickness that had menaced our Count for quite some time as he moved within his class like one of the living dead—("a sickness" can be synonym for "a thought")—you mustn't be amazed to see that sickness now explode in the tremendous fashion we here have been at pains to describe, revealing all of the nobleman's subterranean longing, all his desperate need for an experience of the real. The field and the wooded copse, the dining room and the well, the rapid April clouds and the closeness of November, coming now to confuse themselves the one with the other here at the end of our story, are things then of which you have no need to investigate the cause: recognize them rather to contain the resolute and one true path of the soul among things till now pretending to be the soul, imitating the soul at the cost of great turbulence and fear.

XXI
The Trial Begins

The hearing. At the well again. Almost November.

Before following our gentleman to an invisible part of
the island where the hearing room most probably lay concealed among the roots of an olive or an oak tree, we have to
bear witness to a few weak cries from ABOVE (a proof of the
voyager's confinement to some BELOW), certain sounds of
"Daddo! Daddo! *O senhor conte!*" coming and going in the
upper air before fading finally out, and surely the fruit of the
nobleman's overly sharp sensibility. He was not well, and
knew it; or to put it better, he could "feel" it. A high headi-
ness welled up inside him and the facts that spasmodically
riveted his attention were unrelated to his physical body.
These voices, then, were beyond his ken. He stood there,
looking out into the hall from his dock, and his ear couldn't
hear them; he was wholly engrossed by the happenings in his
most immediate surroundings.

First of all, there was the Judge. On entering the dark,
narrow hall in which the Count had come to find himself, he
had given an order for light, ever more light, an enormity of
light, and the poor Lombard suddenly took in the vision of his
whereabouts.

The hall was quite large, but squalid, just like many
such halls that you are sure to have seen in illustrations of the
famous trials of the nineteenth century, and you can't imag-

ine garments more subdued and colorless than what the people there were wearing. There were women with babies in their arms, and longish men with a look between unemployment and drunkenness. Women, men, and babies were all of them grey, their large eyes lacerated by those rays of neurosis that form a natural part of indigence. In their midst, the down-at-heel lords of Ocaña counted as no exception, if not for their sullen silence. The Count sat on the dock of the accused, and a boy with a sensitive face held him by the hand, wanting to offer comfort. The negligent summer outfit in which he had crossed the sea had vanished from the Count's fine back and he was attired entirely in black: a suit that suited "God's Witness," which were the words emblazoned across it on a wide silver sash. He was ashamed of such clothing, and this added still another impulse to the shudders coursing ceaselessly through his body.

"Be calm, now. . . . They'll get it over with quickly!" The kind-hearted youth saw his way to whispering this phrase in his ear, and was no one other than Ilario.

"It's this suit . . . that makes me feel ashamed," replied the Lombard.

The trial wasn't clear, since no one yet knew the name of God's murderer, nor even if He were truly dead; and this— hope can be just so terrifying—was what made the Count tremble. At any rate, the Hopins could be eliminated. It seemed slightly that Segovia-Mendes might be responsible; other suspicions weighed on someone from Milan; but here again the Count could rest at ease, solidly aware of the enormous piety of his birthplace. The prosecuting attorney, a person quite similar to *senhor* Cole, recounted all the miseries and persecutions heaped on the Creator of the Heavens before He finally expired: where He had slept His agitated nights, how He suffered the lack of air, how His body had covered with sores. The prosecution listed the letters and

173

appeals He had directed to the Milanese authorities and to many of the city's nobles, but all to no avail: the documents had never received the least consideration. Without exception, they had been crumpled up and tossed into waste-paper bins by secretaries.

"Where were the accused?" inquired the Judge, revealing the accused to be plural; so only one had been designated to represent them all.

"On their yachts, sir," answered Cole, drying his eyes with a large red kerchief, and the Count concluded that he was basically good. No longer able to bear the pain of it all, the prosecutor returned to his chair.

The Count imagined that he himself would now be called to offer testimony on the crime, and he raised his hand, in spite of how it trembled, but no one paid him any attention. His eyes burned and he stood erect on his feet, looking around him.

"Bring in the Victim," pronounced the Judge, rising to his feet. The whole hall of quivering, weeping people rose with him.

Two men entered, pushing a white trolley that bore the corpse of the Highest and Most Holy.

Surely you've longed to know the true semblance of this Being whom the centuries have surrounded with fables while leaving us always uncertain of having been faced with the undeniable. What lay there, curled up on a leaf and asleep, was a simple white butterfly.

But what grace it must have had as it hovered over meadows and flowering shrubs before the tremendous event of its death! A simple weak grub, but with the purest wings— wings still trembling (perhaps fluttering with the breathing of the persons in the hall) in an appearance of life. Golden antennae, and miniscule eyes overflowing with goodness, very pure and very sad.

Wondering that so weak and simple a creature, now robbed of life, could contain the secret, the very origins of the immense astounding universe with all its splendors, gifts, and everything that he and other nobles had possessed and enjoyed, the Count became aware of just how unpardonable that murder would always remain, and that the grief of the Constellations was infinite. But at this point, Reader, his resources were very nearly exhausted. His body had begun to weaken already several hours before, and the strength he had found in his indignation wavered within a constantly growing anxiety about the culprit. For a while he cast a stare of tranquil ecstasy at the remains of the Highest and Most Holy and then babbled a few broken phrases in which little could be distinguished: "...others... and so... was here... uselessness...."

After that, he fainted.

While walking towards the well, in hopes of a breath of fresh air, he realized he was being followed. The two Guzmans, very well armed. The Count's soul was laden with so much pain, and his head was reeling with such a strange and terrible drunkenness as to make this the very first time that those ruffians were to leave him entirely unfazed. He might have been walking since time immemorial in a place that eluded all recall, or perhaps in a place where memories were far too abundant, as can happen on certain quiet veiled mornings when you can't quite tell if you're starting into April or looking forward to the month of the dead. He could feel them at his heels and sensed their emotions as far from pacific, yet none of that held any interest for him. He had the sensation of seeing inside of them; they might have been transparent; and what he felt there was a sadness, an immobility, and a heavy rapture, almost the same as his own.

It seemed there was nothing left on the island, neither

the hearing room, nor the house, no matter whether a prison or a royal palace, nor even the boats, down at the bottom of the beach among the brush. There was only the well, and a little woman in tears standing next to it. She was very small, very odd-looking, very poor, but his illness would have kept the poor Count from seeing her even had she been in every way the opposite. He paid her no attention at all. Meanwhile, the two Guzman brothers came abreast of him.

"Has your dear brother departed, gentlemen?" asked the Count. He spoke from the center of a new tranquillity, and his face glowed with a distant smile.

"Yes," replied Felipe, lowering his head.

"Someday *o senhor conte* will forget us too," said Hipolito.

So in fact they loved him, but that no longer struck any resonance in the Count's sad soul.

The little woman to the side of the well began crying "Hee! Hee! Hee!" It suggested a lament. Balancing in the air around her, trying to settle on her rags, were three white butterflies. The miserable creature shooed them away.

"What's the matter with this poor soul?" the sick man inquired, benevolently.

"Human souls can tremble for no good reason, sir; they're like the leaves on trees." replied Hipolito.

"That's quite true."

"Here there was once a beautiful house," observed Felipe. "Time and desperation have left nothing behind. Desperation is a terrible thing, sir."

"Basically, too, it's useless, since God doesn't die . . ." the Count weakly responded, casting a glance around him. "He endlessly multiplies Himself," he remarked, while observing the butterflies, "both God and his priceless grace. You'll see Him rise again some day."

"Yes, *o senhor.*"

There were small white clouds at the top of the sky and the hurricane was over, which they asserted so beautifully: that the hurricane was gone and one needed once again to make a place for great calm and piety.

He walked away, still followed by the Guzmans, though at a respectful distance, and re-entered the Tribunal.

XXII
The Hearing Resumes

The high sky. Identified! Daddo content.

They had finally identified the culprit. The Count's worst fear had come true, since it was someone from Milan: a poor thin youth, tall and green, wearing a green tunic, dripping with streamers of algae. The crushing weight of the accusation had reduced the boy to tears, but the weapon with which he had struck the Lord was still in his hand. One of the bailiffs delicately removed it, and that hand fell back to his side like something inanimate. Mouthing out incessant words and crying, he was the very image of wretchedness. Yet despite his miserable appearance, he had the most beautiful voice in the world: the Count couldn't help admitting it. A silvery voice, very sweet, very pure, an impression of something shattered. The Count felt no pity for him, but the Count was quite weak and it hurt him to look upon suffering, even if he somehow felt, obscurely, that all these sufferings would soon be over and that the assailant too would be overwhelmed with untellable joy since the Highest and Most Holy, notwithstanding his wounds, was still alive. Next to him, the accused, but also next to the Count—they bore quite a striking resemblance—stood the kind Ilario, trying constantly to comfort this shadow of affliction. Close to the sick man's ear he kept repeating, "You'll see, there's nothing at all to worry about, my dear, nothing at all." He spoke in the same mild voice the Count had noticed on first setting foot on the island. But the Count wasn't really concerned about the fate of that man, regardless of what it might be; he was only fascinated by his fall. Indeed, we can fall very low, no matter how highly society has placed us. Contingency lies in ambush behind the greatest stability, and the void in the lee of human glory! Destiny stands suddenly before you!

He saw a group of sailors gathered around the cage, or rather the well, and he felt a twinge akin to disgust as he recognized Salvato.

"The water wasn't very deep, sir," the poor man commented while speaking with Mr. Hopins, "but he took a terrible beating against the walls."

"Lay him down flat! Give him room for air!" cried Mr. Hopins.

That's how they took him to the house, on a stretcher made of a few planks of wood, tied together with cords. The Count could see it distinctly. He saw the sky was very high, and his joy made him smile.

When the hearing resumed, the Tribunal was slightly different (perhaps because of that momentary disorientation that had flooded through the Count). It was a room with tall, very bare walls, and was less intensely illuminated than the real Tribunal. Many people had left, and the hall lay in the sway of a painful silence. Thoughtful and compassionate eyes peered from every side at the accused, who had been stretched out on a cot. You see, Reader, that people have hearts, when everything is said and done, and often brim with goodness: deep down inside, everyone pitied the sudden calamity of the poor man on trial—everyone except the young Count, even though his own heart was far from hard, in fact quite the opposite. During the last several moments he had been taken by a sense of great surprise. He had two sensations—very much in contrast with one another—and he couldn't, at least for the present, find a way of connecting them, despite their sharing an atmosphere of meaning that harbingered nothing terrible and in fact held something happy and human, and therefore reason for hope. He felt his voyaging had all amounted to immobility; and now, in immobility, true voyaging was getting underway. Then he felt that these voyages are dreams, and iguanas are warnings. That there are no iguanas, but only disguises, disguises thought up by human beings for the oppression of their neighbors and then held in place by a cruel and terrifying society. He himself had been product and expression of such a society, but now he was stepping out of it. This made him content.

The hearing resumed, but ran in disorder, and always against the slow, grave background of the bells. The accused's principal guilt seemed to lie in his lack of awareness, a kind of boyishness or melancholic stupor that had left him estranged from the world's harsh reality, and had shown him fables and monsters where there had only been markets and creatures who rated no mention in the register of economic potency. He saw that the accusation—which was presented by the person least authorized to take the floor, meaning Fidenzio Aureliano—brought any number of people to tears. It was something of which all of them were guilty, and without the extenuations of a life of heart-felt charity. A monk whom the Count had never seen before stood up and spoke uninterruptedly for quite some time. He observed that the count's guilt ("so he too, poor devil, is a count!" remarked Daddo to himself, moved to pity), if it were proper to speak of guilt at all, was fundamentally synonymous with his idealism, an idealism with no true awareness of the real, no sense of accountancy and debit and credit. "He didn't see," the monk continued, "that the charm he found so winning in the creatures of the islands had cost them their expulsion from the one authentic paradise, which is the only one we know, located here on the earth and with access conceded on payment of cash money." He enumerated the lands, houses, and islands that people like the count had purchased—and not only the Aleardis, he said, whose domains were beyond calculation, but the Hopins too—bringing about the downfall of gentle souls like Ilario and consigning them to perversion. In result of this power accorded to money, crimes heaped up torture and loneliness as the only lot of whomever had none of it. Even when redeemed by deeds such as the count had performed—descending into the well and shattering the bones of his body while attempting the rescue of the miserable Iguana—such crimes assumed no other name. Extenuating circumstances might nonetheless be held in account by the Celestial Judge, meaning the whole of humanity.

The Count wept.

"So he did do something good," came the further remark, "he . . . so his life was not useless! I thank you, Sir . . . or Gentlemen, whoever you may be. Finally he paid, and with his truest coin! He gave his life for the Iguana!"

Screaming these words—truly a scream—he saw that he was that other count.

He was still in time to hear Ilario's tearful query as to how he felt, and clearly to recognize all the various characters whom this story has described, but they were no longer in any way extravagant. The Count had been healed of his fantasizing mind. They were simple poor souls who live in our world, people like so many others of whom you're certain, Reader, to have made frequent acquaintance: people full of scheming and subterfuge, avid for a rise towards the top of the heap, but not finally evil. He looked at Ilario—no longer the terrible Mendes—and saw a poor sad boy who held him by the hand. With a bittersweet smile, the Count then suddenly LEFT. He felt he needed air.

So he returned to the well, and the two Guzman brothers again stood beside him.

XXIII
The Voyage Resumes

Who the Iguana was.
"Let's go . . . the cosmos . . . grace . . . all of us . . ."

Even though armed, they had the same shabby look they always had, and the Count felt sorry for them.

By now he knew everything about them, how they had grown up, loveless, without teaching, in terrible loneliness; and how they had earlier been children. The childish hopes they had nourished gave him a shearing whir of pain. Yet he was happy at one and the same time. Nothing abates the urgency of a restructuring of the world's economies, but he had rightly understood that life and how we live it are made only of mutability: a voyage towards a larger continent, a gentler reality, free of humiliation and perplexity and the wide-ranging deception with which life attempts to demonstrate that it isn't simply a river or a stream flowing into a sea; but that is all it really is, and there, in that azure quiet, it finds its repose.

The ancient sweetness in the air made him all the more sensitive to this earth that each of us has to abandon— sensitive as well to all of its particulars—and he asked the Guzmans if they had studied when they were boys. He wondered how they had made out at school.

"Not very well, sir," answered Hipolito, drying away a tear.

"But you mustn't cry, my dear," said the Count, "for not

having had good grades. You know, I didn't very much like to study either. With young people, that's how it always is."

There were yellow flowers, in a field, very large. Hipolito picked a few and silently offered them to the Count. He put them on his chest and over his face.

Inside of him, however, remained a certain obscurity. Owing to those flowers, to that yellow vegetal splendor, and equally to the strength of the light in the air, he could no longer see the path they were walking, and then Felipe cried out in a voice he seemed to have heard before:

"Be careful, sir! You could fall!"

He saw her again, quite suddenly.

She was no iguana, nor even a queen. She was a servant girl like so many to be found in the islands, with two large staring eyes in a face no larger than a grain of rice. She had black hair arranged like a little tower around a severe, timid face. An unsmiling mouth. Rather than white lace, she was dressed in simple grey rags. Lying on those rags, scattered all around her like petals of mud, she seemed to be sleeping, dreaming. Her eyes were open and fixed. The water kept rising.

"Perdita!" cried the Count.

He heard a strange, humble voice rise up from the bottom to answer him:

"I'm here, *o senhor conte.*"

"Hold on! I'm coming down."

That was how his descent had begun, and now it was ending.

He reawakened, looked at Ilario, and smiled. He asked, weakly, what time it was.

"Three o'clock," the poor boy replied. The craziness typical of moments of gravity made him want to add "if my watch is running right," but he saw that the Count, closed up in swathes of bandages, was beginning to toss and turn. Ilario could stand it no longer and ran off to hide in the kitchen.

Only the Hopins and the two Avaredo brothers remained beside the Count: the brothers standing, whereas the Hopins had dropped to their knees and lowered their heads, feeling it not a good thing to study a man as he dies . . . but their ears stayed open and listened in amazement to strange, broken words and soft-spoken orders, like "buy . . . by now useless . . . have to look . . . money's not enough . . . those boats there . . . wrong sort of up-bringing . . . hardly matters . . . good weather . . . let's go . . . the cosmos . . . incalculable holdings . . . new lands . . . grace . . . all of us . . ."

The words stopped. A rapid, anxious, continuous sound rattled from the sick man's chest. His face went long and dark, and then, for no apparent cause, serene.

Courteously, just as he had lived, the Count died.

Two hours later, the saddest, most palpable confusion reigned in the miserable village of Ocaña—the village that the Count, in his madness, had never seen. People came and went, asking for news, but the only response returned, unfortunately, lay in the reddened eyes of the island nobles.

Since the evening was stormy and the house, like the village, was without a stock of votive candles, the Hopins brought lanterns from aboard their yacht and lit one in every room for their nightlong wake with the unfortunate Segovia-Guzmans, who cried like lambs.

Another but almost ridiculous lament came from a room not far from the gentleman's, and this was the villa's enchanted little servant. She hadn't done herself a great deal of harm in her attempted suicide, no matter whether real or feigned (only God can judge). Fortune and perhaps a certain benignity of the grasses and waters that fill mysterious wells had come to her assistance. And that wasn't all. Even the wounds of the heart—which you too, Reader, may have experienced—had volatized, disappeared, since the whole of her passionate, savage mind was filled now with the Count's death and the compassion he had shown her: from the moment he had cried "Perdita," all of the island's desperate spells had broken, and even her mischievous perversity had vanished along with them. Seated among her packets and little bags, she consigned herself to tears and desperation. Oh, what she wouldn't have given to reawaken him!

Mrs. Hopins showed commiseration, even though you will remember the lady's ejaculation, "Kill her!" She went to carry the girl a bowl of milk and hot wine. She felt that the Count's death was not the little servant's fault (a feeling, moreover, that everyone shared), and was rather to be attributed to their sophisticated games, which had gone beyond the comprehension of a soul so fresh as he had been. Remorse induced her to a swelling of fellow-feeling of which formerly she would not have believed herself capable.

A great profound silence reigned in the house, despite everyone's being awake; and that was because the Count, after his tragic reawakening, was very peacefully sleeping.

In a kind of oaken boat that his sailor and the two rude brothers had lovingly prepared, he lay in a suit of black evening dress he had never worn before, a briar rose within his slender hands, his elegant feet scattered over with an abundance of yellow flowers. Manrique's book and a silver cross were arranged at the side of his pillow.

The Count had never been calmer or more handsome, which was in keeping moreover with the legend of the Grees; but there was also something else in that fine white face, a touch of some darkness like a shadow of what the nobleman had suffered in his last two days of existence while tortured by presentiments of evil and suspicions on the true identities of culprits: that shadow seemed still to persecute him. Everything had been clarified, but perhaps his memory could still cast that veil, lighter than a breath, that came and went across his sensitive forehead. Equally, it might have been an effect of the uncertain flames. But he also wore an indisputable smile that just barely lifted the corners of his lips; for this marvelous smile of those who have but recently surmounted the lesser of the trials (the other is life), there seemed no reason at all.

Everyone present was deeply moved by that smile and it made them participants in who knows what summit of the glory of the world, no matter that the world is so commonly taken for merchandize, or something even less. The smile ended with the arrival of dawn.

The voyager seemed more tired, and somehow secretive.

It was raining.

XXIV
The Chapel by the Sea

Letters from Ocaña. Winter. A crude invitation.

You too, Reader, will have noticed how the facts of life that most approach sublimity tend to come to mean conclusions, or at best to pass unobserved, making way for trifles that literally leave the community breathless. When Milan received word that the Count would never return, all the city's newspapers were accordingly arage with a question we'd judge to be of slight importance: whether or not automobiles should be permitted to park in the area behind the Duomo (a question already a thousand times tabled and resuscitated, proving the urgency of finding a solution). So news of the tragedy appeared on a last page beneath the hasty caption: THE ALEARDI HOME IN MOURNING. That was all. If society's response to a person's death can indicate that person's previous social worth, one saw that the Count, despite aura and possessions, had been a nobody, and he had been brought to that pass by his curious mediocrity. To say nothing of being feared, he hadn't even been loved. Even Adelchi was distracted. He might have had more reason than others to feel distress and show concern, but his days were a maddening whirl around an overwhelming prospect of unexpected, quite conspicuous capital backing, which in fact, parenthetically, came about and promptly transformed his life. He was sorry to learn his friend would not be coming back, but he postponed mourning to some future when he wouldn't be so busy. Such a future, unfortunately, never presented itself.

For mother, her Ladyship the Countess, there were no perplexities: she had long since seen the signs of the moral disintegration of her son, and his assaults against the family fortune had dug a chasm between them even if he himself had remained unaware of it. She was prepared to lose him. But that didn't hold for the emerald, which was one of the family's most prideful gems. She summoned her lawyers, saw to being received at the Curia (business she had to attend to in Switzerland left travelling out of the question), and arranged for a letter to be written to Lisbon, with Lisbon in turn dispatching a party of priests to the unfortunate island, where the emerald was quite easily recovered. Bosio had established residence in the house and found it simply by paying a visit to the kitchen. It was behind the box of salt, where Felipe had placed it, never suspecting that the stone had such great value. Bosio himself reported back, composing a lengthy letter in which he offered her Ladyship reconfirmation of his long-standing devotion to the Aleardi household, and added, in such a light, that he hoped to receive instructions for the repatriation of the gentleman's mortal remains, since this island was no fit place for an Aleardi's final repose. The Countess replied in her own hand that she would see to everything, but that Aleardo, in any case, had already ceased to be her son well prior to his death, and the best she could do was to pray for him. She sent money for masses, and her last envoy of a thousand lire was dated November seventh. Then nothing more. As she returned on the tenth from Berne, her automobile overturned and the gentlewoman died.

For Bosio, whose sensibility took very little pleasure in the continuing presence of such a reminder of the Count, other adequate solutions were easily envisioned, but on referring his idea to the Guzman brothers, he understood from their curt, "No, sir," that it was better not to insist.

Daddo had been buried in the southern part of the island, on a stretch of land adjacent to the beach, very isolated. Bosio, moreover, desired somehow to protect himself from the sight of the place, which he unfailingly encountered on his walks, and ordered it enclosed within a chapel which made it even more solitary. The brothers, however, furtively fitted out the little construction with a window that faced the open waters. Only the confused waves of the sea, as they fold back over themselves in the mystery of the sunset, possessed an unobstructed view into the chapel's emptiness. Going there when the tide was low and their mood was sad, the two young men never heard any resemblance of a fresh, open laugh or a pitying voice; nor when they would peep into the white interior did they ever see some shining figure collected in meditation. No one was ever there, as was right, since goodness and grace do not belong to this world; and once they have tearfully left this world behind, God never inflicts them with the sorrow of having to return.

He was now removed to some great distance away from them and perhaps had even forgotten them, yet the Guzman brothers were never to forget him. You will have understood that their mask of cruelty concealed a heart much deeper than those of many others. One can say that their perennial memory of the Count brought about a change in their lives.

Two other people had changed as well. Segovia, by now in Caracas, was a serene if not happy husband dedicated entirely to the care of his immense terrains. He had abandoned all writing and turned into a wise, calm man, maybe a bit portly and with a slight drift towards pessimism, but the presence of his wife could keep such things on an even keel. He went to church every morning at dawn and briefly confessed the venial sins of which all of us are guilty; afterwards he found himself renewed and took Communion. Hoping to meet the Count again some day in a more disinterested world, he found his measure of peace.

The other person to have changed was the island's servant, but here, Reader, you will have to excuse us. Something prevents us from speaking of her directly—perhaps the knowledge of how much the Count had loved her, and of how the poor soul's back passed constantly curved among the silent horrors of the world. So we have to be content with recording a few passages from certain letters sent off in the course of last October from Ocaña's "Petit Hotel": letters from a Mrs. Rubens, the wife of a jeweller in Lyle, to her husband who had remained in France:

". . . concerning the amusements you allude to, my dear, I'm afraid you have a wrong idea. The air here is quite fresh, but the place is terribly sad. The hotel I write you from is the island's only lodgings, and is cute but empty. If the Catholic priest who had it built was thinking to make any money, or to inspire people's souls to some desire for purification, well, I'd say he has missed his mark. To my way of thinking, the first complaint is the lack of decent service. The two 'geezers' I've told you about aren't the only illustrious scoundrels on the island. There are others too . . . and there is also a servant girl I don't like a bit. She could be any age at all, a hag or an infant. You just can't tell because of how she does her hair. An instinctive discourtesy combined with a little forgetfulness is quite enough to cancel out any of the qualities (quite unlikely) that this little person may possess. You look at her—and her eyes, really, are just a pool of black light, they're just that fixed and sweet—and you could even think she's nice, but then you catch on that she never looks at you at all. She's always looking, sort of behind you, at something missing that's never coming back. A thing

191

like that gives you a funny, unpleasant feeling. The priest
says she's retarded, but I'd call her mad—one of those miserable, hopeless cases compounded of pride and a bad personality, which is why these islands are so incurably poor. And
they tell me—imagine this!—that she's in love with a count,
and he made some silly remark that has gotten it into her
head that he's coming back to marry her, whereas the truth,
from what I've heard, is that he has already been married
for years. Could anything be more pitiful? . . ."

From another letter:

" . . . now I've gone to visit the tomb of this famous lover
they tell me was a count who came here and died—which was
something I didn't know—and it's all very obscure. Other
tourists too—in seasons better than it is right now—go to
visit it, but nobody at all was there today except for our
servant girl. Such a disrespectful attitude she had! So
there's no room left for any of my illusions. I found her
next to the wall of the chapel just sitting there with a little
mirror in one hand and a comb in the other. She was doing
her hair! And God knows why, but she seemed so perfectly
pleased with herself. Then she saw me, my dear, and
started laughing, and such a stupid laugh, but still so
cunning, like she was certain she's some great beauty. I
finally saw just how inhuman her heart really is, and thoroughly insensitive to everything. And people here say
she's compassionate! These people, *chéri*, are really disturbing. They're as changeable as the ocean, and very
tough, and nothing moves them, except maybe for money
(though I do try to be careful). You talk to them and they
never answer. That's all they have on their minds: *l'ar-
gent!* Isn't that humiliating?"

And from a final letter:

"I'm about to leave now, and I have to confess being left amazed by something that's happened: I've found all my tips exactly where I left them along with a note on the night table. Maybe they can't read. Or did they think my tips were too small? There's really no way of understanding what they want! Forgive me, dear, if I've bored you, but this Ocaña is really a very depressing place, with this continuous ocean noise, and black clouds always back and forth across the sky, and being surrounded by *ces muffles*.... Really impossible. Bosio will be leaving on my same boat, which gets in at five from Lisbon and then goes straight back (but only in the summer, and starting tomorrow in fact it won't land here any more). From what I've gathered, he's a very tired man and needs a little civil company, and he seems disappointed with something, but I couldn't say what. I imagine it's unlikely Ocaña will be seeing him again, unlikely too that the Petit Hotel will be seeing any new clients...."

Later:

"I can tell you I am really very sorry I didn't bring along some sweaters, the way you told me to. It's quite cold here now, and it will be worse at sea.... '*September is far away....*' The only people left here are the Guzmans and the servant girl, of whom they appear to be quite fond.... People, at bottom, that have to be pitied. But the boat now is coming in.... See you soon, *chéri*...."

This was the third winter to return to Ocaña after the facts of the story we've told, and when the last of the pension's guests, along with the figure of the bizarre don Bosio, had taken the route leading back again to civilization, no one

193

remained on the island—leaving aside a few obscure villagers—except for the personnel of the Petit Hotel, who were people far wiser and better than appearances made it easy to believe. By now, they had little work to do, if any, and when they returned towards evening to the house, they spent the rest of their time (often far into the night if it was raining or if the wind was up) in an occupation no one would have imagined, least of all the vivacious Mrs. Rubens, thinking back to their mute figures and blind silences. They were learning, Reader, to read and write, with a great deal of difficulty, but mutually assisting each other with a great deal of love. They were certain, among their efforts, not only of paying tribute to their dear distant poet (they never abandoned their illusion of his greatness), but also of someday being able to direct some missive to the Count, whose immortality they found beyond question. The girl, whose health was never good and who was always inattentive, never excelled in her studies, even though she desired to do so with all the humble force of her heart, whereas the *uncles*, as she had been calling these other good servants now for quite some time, had already made real progress. . . . It was mainly for her, to give her a sense of peace and joy and to allow her a renewed relationship with her idol, that the two of them one night wrote the following crude poem. Here it is, and as persons of culture you're to be asked to forgive them for their awkwardness.

INVITATION WRITTEN BY THE GUZMAN BROTHERS FOR LOVE OF THE IGUANA—SO THAT THE COUNT'S IMMORTAL SOUL—WILL BE ENCOURAGED TO REMEMBER OCAÑA:

Presentation of the place

This is the sea!
This is the sky
Grey and yellow
Rain and cold.

True and proper invitation

I

Help me.
Know me.
Greet me.
Call me by my name,
not by the serpent's.
I want to come to life again.

II

Count of Milan
you are not to wait,
I don't want emeralds,
I want to be
compassionate and just,
like you.

III

Dear my lord,
good and compassionate!
Grand Constable, for love of the King,
of Charles the Fifth,
save Spain
and Portugal,
the vanquished countries
asleep
in the algae
in the stone
in the mountain
in Meseta
and Murcia,
in Estremadura.
Save the bull,
the cow, the lamb.
Save the pilgrim.
Bring the light,
bring the sun,
water and gardens.

IV

Count of Christ
you are not to resist.
Come to the well,
there is no water.
There are no flowers,
there is no one.
There is silence.
The serpent weeps.
The crouching frog.

There is fear.
Bring the light.
Bring the sun.
Without judgment
they have judged us.
Look into the well.
If you call us
we will answer.

V

We are not dead.
It is November.
Yellow and red,
the sun rises
from the cistern.
We tremble.

VI

Save the bull.
Protect the cow
and the lamb
and the falling
star.

Salutation

You will remain
dear count
in Estremadura
you will look at us
from above the mountains,
crying out.

These verses, if we can call them verses, made a certain little person break into laughter, since that was the only way, if not for others that were even stranger, in which she could ever express the force of her feelings, the force—as Mrs. Rubens had put it—of her heart's inhuman depth.

And with that, dear Reader, we will take our leave, like Bosio and others of greater fortune, from Ocaña and its humble human family. And if you are surprised by the sea that closes so easily over these evils and these smiles, and over the figure of a dark-minded gentleman, or by time that endlessly passes, in Milan as in the islands, pulling everything into its wake and directed towards eternity, then please remember Unamuno's pressing question and the similar questions you yourself have asked, and you will see that at least this sense of surprise remains the same.